BASES FULL!

BASES FULL

BASES FULL!

RALPH HENRY BARBOUR

Published by Wildside Press.

Visit us online at wildsidepress.com.

INTRODUCTION
KARL WURF

Ralph Henry Barbour (1870–1944) was one of the most prolific American writers of juvenile sports fiction during the late nineteenth and early twentieth centuries. Born in Cambridge, Massachusetts, Barbour came of age at a time when organized team sports were beginning to dominate school and college life. His stories captured this new athletic culture with energy and optimism, presenting games like football, baseball, and crew not only as contests of skill but as tests of loyalty, discipline, and fair play. Over his long career, he produced more than one hundred novels and many short stories, shaping the sports story genre for generations of young readers.

Barbour's early influences came from two traditions. First, the school story model established by British authors such as Thomas Hughes in *Tom Brown's Schooldays* gave him a framework for portraying academic institutions as training grounds for character. Second, the rise of American local-color fiction and adventure writing in the late nineteenth century encouraged lively depictions of regional life and practical realism. Blending these models, Barbour created his own distinctive voice, one that combined vivid game scenes with tales of friendship, perseverance, and moral growth.

In addition to his independent novels, Barbour also worked in collaboration. With L. H. Bickford, he published light romances under the pseudonym Richard Stillman Powell, most notably *Phyllis in Bohemia* (1897). Though these departures show his versatility, it was his sports fiction that secured his reputation. His ability to dramatize the strategies of play while weaving in the personal struggles of boys at school set him apart from his contemporaries and established him as a foundational figure in American juvenile literature.

Barbour's place in literature rests on the way he bridged entertainment and instruction. His stories mirrored the cultural belief that athletics built character and prepared young men for the challenges of adulthood. In the process, he helped codify the "sports story" as a recognizable genre in popular publishing. Publishers such as D. Appleton & Co. relied on his editorial guidance for sports manuals and fiction alike, reflecting his authority both as a storyteller and as a curator of athletic knowledge.

The breadth of Barbour's sports novels ensured that nearly every major school and college game found its chronicler. His stories often featured underdogs rising to meet decisive moments, echoing the American fascination with perseverance and fair competition. Generations of readers found in his pages both the thrill of the contest and the reassurance that values like teamwork, honor, and determination mattered as much as the scoreboard.

For readers interested in exploring Barbour's other sports novels, several stand out as close companions to *Bases Full!*. *The Half-Back* (1899) was among his earliest successes and set the pattern for many later works. *Captain of the Crew* (1901) and *Behind the Line* (1902) vividly portray school and college athletics, while *Weatherby's Inning* (1903) and *The Crimson Sweater* (1905) showcase his mastery of baseball and football settings. Later titles such as *Left End Edwards* (1914), *For Yardley* (1911), and *The Fighting Scrub* (1924) demonstrate his enduring interest in team play and individual growth. Together, these works confirm Barbour's enduring place as one of the foremost chroniclers of American youth in sport.

CHAPTER I
THE WINNING GOAL

"Shoot! Shoot!"

The Wyndham forwards had swept down the rink, successfully eluding Wolcott's defense, and now Captain Cooper slid the puck gently to the left as the enemy point checked desperately, and from the audience, for the moment forgetting chilled feet and numbed fingers, the shout came exultantly, imploringly:

"Shoot! Shoot!"

Ogden took the pass, but a Wolcott wing slashed wildly at his stick and the defending cover point dashed back to the beleaguered goal and the chance was gone. Ogden did shoot, but the puck struck the end of the net and a Wolcott skater hooked it to him and, pursued by Ogden, swept behind the goal. A fracas in the further corner followed and then a brown-legged player was off down the rink and Wyndham hastened to cover.

It was the last period and only a few minutes remained. The score was still a tie at 6 to 6. The visiting team had started the game in whirlwind fashion, scoring twice before the Blue had found its pace. Then Wyndham had tallied on a lift from near the center of the rink by Raiford, and that lucky shot had nerved the home team to faster play. Wolcott had scored a third tally from a furious mix-up in front of goal when the rubber had slid from someone's skate and edged past a corner of the net. At 3 to 1 the game had stayed until, close to the end of the period, Wyndham, using a five-man attack, had overwhelmed the adversary and netted a clean shot from directly in front of the goal. Captain Cooper, Wyndham's right wing, had put that in.

After the intermission Wolcott had again forced the fighting, and Craigie, goalkeeper for the home team, had been fairly battered with the puck until at last it got by him for Wolcott's fourth score. Coach Hilliard had substituted Cowden for Jensen at cover point then, and subsequently the enemy had experienced more difficulty in reaching shooting distance. Cowden had proved himself more alert than his predecessor on attack, as well, and Wyndham's next tally was a result of his "get away" followed by a quick backward pass to Raiford and a sizzling shot from a hard angle. Wyndham had again scored less than a minute later when Captain Cooper had taken the puck into enemy territory, skating along the boards, and, after bowling over the outer defense, passed to Raiford in front of point and then, when the center slid it back to him, slipped it craftily past the goalkeeper's feet with a mere flick of his stick.

From 4 to 4 the score had leaped quickly to 6 to 6, each team winning alternate goals. Couch, Wyndham's point, had been sent off for illegal checking and a Wolcott forward for loafing off-side. Jeff Adams, who had taken Couch's position, had proved an improvement, for, although light, he had broken up several attacks. Still later Coles had relieved Cragie at goal. Now, with the score still even and only a handful of minutes to play, all indications pointed toward an extra period. Wyndham wanted to win today's contest, for it was the deciding test in the three-game series with her old rival—Wolcott Academy. Wyndham had lost the first, played on her home rink, but had romped off with the second, played at Cotterville. So far this school year the Dark Blue had proved supreme in football and had been defeated in basketball; the deciding contest of the latter sport was still only a week old. A victory in hockey would atone for the basketball repulse; indeed, more than atone, since at both Wyndham and Wolcott hockey was a major sport and basketball a minor. Besides, Wolcott had carried off the hockey palm last winter, and while that fact might be forgotten by many of the onlookers it was well remembered by the players.

Sitting on the bench, sweatered and blanketed, Clifton Bingham cast increasingly anxious glances toward the coach. Clif was only a substitute left wing; whether a first or second substitute he had never been able to determine; but he had taken his place in four of the eleven games played since ice had formed on the little pond and hadn't done so badly. That was Clif's opinion, at least. It was also the opinion, perhaps, not wholly unprejudiced, of Messrs. Kemble and Deane, who, with Clif, constituted what they themselves termed "The Triumvirate," an offensive and defensive coalition of a month's standing. It was undoubtedly natural that Messrs. Kemble and Deane should think well of their comrade's hockey and that they should say so, and it was just as natural that Clif who, in spite of inherent modesty, liked to think well of himself and his deeds, should be impressed by their judgment. But what bothered Clif sometimes was that admiration for his hockey playing seemed not to extend to the coach. The coach was "Pinky" Hilliard, instructor in modern languages and Junior English. "Pinky" was new at this job. As an assistant football coach he had made good for several years, but not until last December had he been selected by a puzzled Athletic Committee to take charge of the hockey team. Good hockey coaches, unlike football or baseball coaches, don't grow on every bush! But Mr. Hilliard had done well.

There was no doubt as to that. After a poor start, the team had entered the third week in January and a winning streak simultaneously, and since the Lovell game, the third consecutive defeat, had come triumphantly through seven contests, losing only the first game with Wolcott. Just the same, in Clif's opinion at least, Pinky was handicapped by one fault: he was blind—or perhaps near-sighted—to the abilities of Clifton Cobb Bingham, Third Class. Not that Pinky hadn't used Clif, for he had; there had been the Horner game in which Clif had, miraculously as it seemed to him, shot a clean goal from a forty-degree angle just before the enemy point had sent him rolling over on the ice. And two or three other games, as well, in one of which he had also scored, although less spectacularly. But here it was the last contest of the year, the biggest game of the big games, and the time was almost up! And Ogden was still playing left wing and Clif Bingham was still huddling on the bench with his skates in a snowbank and his stick clasped by gloved but slowly congealing fingers. Clif, hazarding another glance at the coach's rapt but calm countenance, reflected that the other two members of the Triumvirate were going to be seriously displeased with Pinky if he didn't soon recall the existence of a certain substitute!

Play stopped while the Wolcott cover point and captain recovered from the effects of a violent collision with the boards and the Wyndham team gathered panting about Captain Cooper and indulged in hurried, low-voiced conversation. Clif watched and speculated and hoped that Cooper would notice him; and then, lest he might seem to be courting recognition, relapsed against the back of the bench, partly obscuring himself behind Joe Hanbury's broad bulk. Some one further along the bench asked about the time and Mr. McKnight, timekeeper, responded callously with "Four minutes and twenty seconds!" Gee only four minutes! Clif leaned forward again into sight. So did at least five other youths. This was no time for reticence! Captain Cooper pushed from the group and skated toward the barrier. Planting his stick in the bank of snow beyond it, he leaned forward and spoke to Pinky. Clif couldn't hear what he said, but when the captain's eyes swept along the huddled, blanketed line on the bench he met them squarely. Perhaps Cooper had been seeking someone beyond Clif, but his gaze stopped. For an instant he stared back at Clif, still talking. Then he smiled very suddenly and nodded. Ever after that Clif insisted that Cooper had the most wonderful smile in all the world! Coach Hilliard leaned forward and his gaze, too, rested on Clif. Then he said something else to Cooper and waved a hand, and Clif, arising suddenly, tripped over his stick and fell across the barrier. Both Cooper and Pinky were grinning when Clif reached them, although they pretended they weren't.

"Left wing, Bingham," said the coach. "Watch Houston and cover him close every minute. Go in and see if you can beat him. Don't be afraid of smashing into him. He can't hurt you. All right, Ogden! That's enough!"

Clif was over the boards in record time, shorn of his blanket but still battling with a reluctant sweater. A kind-hearted schoolmate reached across the barrier and helped him out of it; Clif panted "Thanks!" and swung off, tapping his stick, trying hard to get his cold muscles limbered up in the brief moments remaining. Afraid of Houston! Where did Pinky get that stuff, he wondered. He wasn't afraid of the whole Wolcott team. Of course, they might be better than he; skate better, handle their sticks better, shoot better; but they couldn't any of them *try* harder!

The Wolcott captain, once more on his skates, ambled groggily about, watched anxiously by his team mates, and at last signified his desire to continue hostilities. The referee skated away from the boards and lifted his whistle. Players hurried to positions. There was a shrill twe-e-et and the battle went on. Wolcott snared the puck from the face-off and shot along the ice, forming quick formation. Cover point went over to the left, tried desperately to stop the hurtling disk and found himself passed. The attack swept into goal. Clif hovered about Houston, but the puck went across to the other side and there was a quick shot. Coles slipped to the right and the disk bounded away from a leg guard. Clif pushed toward it, but Raiford swung past and hooked it. A Wolcott player challenged him and Raiford fed the puck down the rink. Skates ground and clanged as the teams sped in pursuit. The audience, mostly home-team sympathizers, yelled continuously. The puck shot hither and yon, back and forth, banged against the boards, flew through the air, skimmed the ice, yet remained safely away from both nets. Precious moments sped. Time and again overeagerness brought the shrill whistle for off-side. Both Blue and Brown were striving desperately now, sacrificing science for main force. The playing grew more and more ragged as it became harder. Teamwork almost disappeared, in spite of the captains' frantic appeals, and individual effort, save for brief flashes of cohesion, took the place of formation play. One minute passed and another. The period entered its final two and still the game was undecided and, from all indications, likely to remain so until an extra "sudden-death" period arrived.

Clif had followed instructions implicitly, holding to the tall, fast-skating and elusive Houston like a limpet. The big brown-hosed right wing had more than once showed impatience and more than once vented his wrath by ungentle administrations of his stick against Clif's legs. But Clif didn't feel the blows; at least not then. He continued to dog Houston's every move, and such covering, while it mitigated against Clif's usefulness as an attacking player, certainly mitigated quite as much against Houston's value in a similar capacity. Twice at least Clif was able to tell himself with grim satisfaction that his close attention to the big Wolcott chap had prevented a shot.

Captain Cooper stole the puck close to the Wolcott goal and set off with it, alone for the moment and unaided, while shrill shouts and yells of triumph hailed his progress. Dodging right and left, skating from side to side of the rink, he eluded the enemy defenders until, at last, he had an unchallenged shot. Just before a Wolcott man plunged at him he slammed the puck viciously at the net. But the Brown's goalkeeper threw himself in front of it and it rebounded, and before a second Wyndham player could reach it the Wolcott point had whipped the disk to the boards and another attempt had failed.

There was a frantic struggle for possession in the corner and then the disk went flying back up the rink to be knocked down by Cowden who, in spite of a hundred protests, fed it back to the forwards. It was Houston who tried for the puck, touched but missed it and put Clif on-side. Clif hooked the rubber from just in front of Houston's reaching blade, slid it to the right for a team mate to take, saw to his consternation that no team mate was there and so went after it again himself. Houston was beside him, very free with his stick, but Clif only blinked when the blows met his shin guards, and pulled the puck toward him.

What happened after that will always remain a great mystery to Clif. To his surprise the puck was in front of him, traveling right, left, straight ahead, at the direction of his stick. But surprise lasted only an instant. Then came chaos. He was threatened in front and from the right, forced to the boards, forced away from them, half checked once. Yet by some marvelous chance the little hard-rubber disk lay always right at the tip of his stick. Somehow he kept his feet, he who had so often fallen ingloriously with far less excuse, and somehow he wormed and dodged and battered his way to the Wolcott goal. At the last moment, when cries from Cooper and from Raiford imploringly urged him to pass, he slid the puck a yard to the left, staggered under the impact of the point's desperate check, whirled precariously around on one skate and, the goalkeeper's scowling countenance looming large and close, made a despairing sweep with his stick. After that he crashed against an iron of the net, rebounded, and slid across the ice in a sitting position until brought up by the boards. But the goal umpire had flung up a hand, Wyndham was shrieking like mad and to Clif, still dazed, came the sweet knowledge that the puck had been caged and that the Dark Blue team had won!

CHAPTER II
THE TRIUMVIRATE

As though realizing that, with the end of the hockey schedule, his services were no longer needed, King Frost retired three days after the Wolcott game. Wyndham awoke to find a warm sun in full command and the earth exceedingly moist and squishy. Little rills flowed along the edges of the paths, water dripped from the roofs, and from all sides, if one listened, came the chuckling murmur of awakening spring. That evening, after supper, the Triumvirate assembled in a first floor room of East Hall. There was nothing unusual in this, however, since the Triumvirate did the same thing almost every evening. There was a full attendance, not a member being absent. Had the secretary—supposing there was one—called the roll it would have gone like this:

"Clifton Cobb Bingham."

"Here!"

"Loring Deane."

"Here!"

"Thomas Ackerman Kemble."

"Uh-huh!"

But there wasn't any secretary. Nor any other officers. Nor, for that matter, any organization. One evening shortly after the holidays, Tom, commenting on the unfailing regularity with which he and Clif adjourned from Dining Hall to Loring's room, added: "Anybody would think this was a sewing circle or a club or something."

"Let's have it a club," suggested Clif. "The East Hall Literary and Recreation Club."

"I'd like to know what's literary about it," Tom objected.

"I am. You and Loring play chess and I read his books. Well, if you don't like that, how about making it a secret organization? Call it the D. K. B."

"What's that stand for?" asked Tom suspiciously. "Don't Kome Back or—"

"Those are our initials, dumbbell."

"Oh! Well, that sounds all right, but—"

"We might call it the Club of Three," offered Loring. "Or—wait a minute! What's the word for three? Trio? No, tri—triumvirate! The Triumvirate! What's wrong with that?"

"Great! It sounds important," said Tom. "Only, before I accept membership I want to ask one simple question. Are there any dues?"

"No dues, no initiation fee! A strictly fraternal, non-partisan, offensive and defensive alliance! 'One for all and all for one!'"

"That's in *The Three Muskeneers*," said Tom.

"The Three—*what*?" asked Clif.

Tom repeated the information. "You know, the story about the three guys—only there were four of 'em—who—"

"*The Three Guardsmen*," interrupted Loring gravely.

"Well, I've always heard it called *The Three Muskeneers*. A fellow named Dumas wrote it. That the same one?"

"Quite," said Loring, and Clif said: "I like your title better, though, Tom."

"What's the matter with it? If you're so smart I can show you the book in the library. I've got it at home, too. I guess I know!"

"Sure it isn't '*Musketeers*' instead of '*Muskeneers*'?"

"Huh? Is it? Heck, I always did wonder what a muskeneer was! Well—" Tom leaned back, grinning—"I never was much on literature! If you don't believe me, ask Mr. Wyatt!"

So that is how the Triumvirate started. It was a sonorous, mouth-filling word, and they liked it. Of course, it was only a joke, yet after a week or two they began to sort of believe in it and lost the habit of smiling when they spoke of it. In some manner it came to be accepted that the borrowed slogan of "One for all, all for one!" meant what it said, and while no opportunity had yet presented that called on them metaphorically to draw swords from scabbards and stand shoulder to shoulder against a common enemy, still the spirit was there.

This evening, which, to be quite exact, was the evening of the twenty-sixth day of February, Tom, noting that the chessboard had not been set out, looked an inquiry and Loring smiled apologetically. "Let's not play tonight, Tom," he said, "if you don't mind. Wattles beat me just before supper, and now I'd rather do something I've got a show at; such as talk. You know they say that conversation is fast becoming a lost art."

"Heck," said Tom, "I haven't noticed it. And you wouldn't think so if you'd heard 'Alick' chewing the rag to me this afternoon. Gosh, I'll bet that guy invented conversation! He knows more words than the dictionary, and he sure can string them together!"

"What," inquired Clif, smiling, "was the subject of Mr. Wyatt's talk?"

"Aw, shut up," growled Tom. "Say, honest, fellows, what's the good of learning about a lot of queers that died a hundred years ago? This Washington Irving, for one. What did he ever do for the Republican Party?"

"Don't you like his stuff?" asked Clif maliciously. "Why, I'm getting an awful kick out of it!"

Tom said "Humph!" disgustedly and Loring chuckled. "Tom's what you might call a Modernist," said the latter. "He prefers his literature fresh, like his rolls. He finds no pleasure in stale bread."

"I'll say I don't," concurred Tom heartily. "Of course some of the old-timers weren't so punk. That guy Dumas, for instance. And Shakespeare. Shakespeare's stuff has a lot of punch generally, but you've got to buckle down to it. Gosh, they must have had a heap of time in those days, the way they spread the words around!"

"Probably got paid by the word," suggested Clif.

"Some of them must have made a pile of dough, then! Alick would have been rich, too, if he'd lived in Shakespeare's time. I'll bet that, at five cents a word, he touched me for a hundred dollars this afternoon!"

"Why don't you study your English Lit," asked Clif, "and not have to listen to Mr. Wyatt's homilies?"

"Study! Heck, I do study! I read all the stuff he tells us to, but it doesn't *mean* anything. I had a hunch the first time I set eyes on that chap that I wasn't going to like him."

"That's a whopper," said Clif. "You do like him, Tom. What you don't like is his line."

"Same thing," grumbled Tom. "I wish I'd been born a Frenchman or a Slovak or—or something so I wouldn't have to dig through all this rot."

"Well, you take my advice, Tom, and get cozy with Alick before you try baseball. Remember what happened last November!"

"I'm not likely to forget," answered the other moodily. "That doddering Ancient Mariner almost queered me for football. If it hadn't been for you fellows—" Tom stopped and shook his head eloquently. "That experience absolutely soured me on sailors, and I've never been able to cheer for the president since."

"The president?" asked Loring, puzzled.

"He's got the name wrong," laughed Clif. "Coleridge, Tom, and not Coolidge wrote *The Ancient Mariner*."

"Coleridge? Well, I guess it's the same name, only spelled differently."

"What I don't understand," said Clif, "is how you manage to get good marks in your other courses and fall down flat in English."

"Because there's some sense to the other stuff, you poor prune! Anyone can see that he's got to know math and history and—well, yes, even Latin, although I'm not strong for it. But, man to man, Loring, what's it going to get me to know about a loony old guy like that 'Ancient Mariner' or read this *Sketch Book* twaddle by Irving? Why didn't he stick to acting instead of—"

"Tom, you'll be the death of me yet!" gasped Clif.

"What did I say then?" demanded Tom indignantly. "You give me a pain, both of you!" But he grinned as though to signify that the pain wasn't acute.

When he had stopped laughing Loring said: "Speaking of baseball, doesn't practice start this week?"

"Thursday," agreed Clif.

"Are you going out?"

"Yes. So is Tom."

"I don't know yet if I am or not," said Tom. "What's the good of it if I get in wrong with Alick and have to quit when the season's half through?"

"Don't get in wrong," advised Clif cheerfully.

"Huh, that's easy enough to say!"

"You'd better," said Loring. "Clif can't be the whole team, you know."

"I'll be lucky if I get a place," said Clif; "any sort of a place. I've played some, but I'm not really much good, and I guess I'm likely to find myself in fast company here."

"Heck," said Tom, "I guess the bunch isn't so wonderful. I notice that they got a lot of wallopings last spring. I may not try for their old team, but if I do try you can bet I'll make it."

"Modest, shrinking little violet, isn't he?" asked Clif of Loring. "Hates himself to death, eh?"

"That's all right," said Tom, "but I've seen some of the guys who made the nine last year, and if I can't play as good ball as they can I'll—I'll—"

"Quit?" suggested Clif. "Well, I haven't your confidence, old son, and if Mr. Connover lets me stick around on the second I'll say 'Thank you.'"

"I've heard," remarked Loring, "that 'Steve' is a pretty good coach."

"I guess he is," said Tom. "Anyway, he made a mighty good football coach last fall when 'Cocky' went to the first. If he can coach the nine as well as he coached the old Fighting Scrub he will be a humdinger. Steve didn't know an awful lot of football, but you wouldn't have suspected it, eh, Clif?"

"He knew enough," answered Clif. "If I had my way I'd wait a couple of weeks before reporting for practice; cut out the gym stuff; swinging clubs and all that; but they say he doesn't like you to report late."

"I guess the gym stuff's good for you," said Tom. "Loosens up the old muscles, you know. Me, I'll be there for the whole awful program."

"Thought you said you didn't know," Clif chuckled.

"Well," answered Tom with entire composure, "I make up my mind quick. I've decided to play since I said that. I'm going to try for second base."

"I shall like that," remarked Clif. "You'll be where I can look out for you while I'm pitching. I'd hate to have you in the outfield, Tom. No telling what awful things you'd do."

"But you're not going to try—" began Loring incredulously.

"Him?" jeered Tom. "He couldn't pitch down Oak Street without breaking a window!"

"Exaggerated, Tom, but containing a modicum of truth," acknowledged Clif. "But let me tell you, old son, that I've got as good a show to pitch for Wyndham as you have to play second base!"

"Is that so? Well, you just wait and see. Listen—"

And while they listen let's look them over, since for the next four months we are going to see a good deal of them. Clifton Bingham—introductions demand formality—was sixteen years of age—an age which, by the way, was that of the other two occupants of the room, although Tom was close to seventeen and Loring was Clif's senior by three months. Clif was tall for sixteen—sixteen and a half, to be more exact—and rather slender. You wouldn't have called him thin, though. He had the appearance of being well-conditioned and looked as though he might be fast; which he was. Good-looking without calling for the word handsome—a word which fellows of his age detest when applied to one of their sex—he owed his attractiveness more to expression than features. The latter were clean-cut, but a critical eye could have found fault with them. He looked alert and he had a smile that you would have liked immensely. He had made right end on the school team late in the season. Like the other members of the Triumvirate, he had entered Wyndham last September and was in the third class.

Mr. Thomas Ackerman Kemble was also a football player and had captained last fall's scrub before he had been elevated, like Clif at the last moment, to a half-back's position on the big team. He was very good looking; I had almost said handsome before I had thought; with the sort of skin from which the tan never quite goes, very dark gray eyes and brown hair that verged closely on the copper. In height he was half an inch, perhaps, shorter than Clif, and he was perceptibly heavier without being large. That half inch was not apparent since he was extraordinarily straight of body and carried himself so that he could have spared another half inch and still seemed as tall as the other. Tom's chin was rather assertive, but in spite of that he was as good-natured and big-hearted as a mastiff; and, like a good many good-natured fellows, he could be extremely stubborn.

I have left Loring Deane to the last, which, since he happens to be the host, is scarcely polite. But Loring requires rather more description than his friends, and one is likely to postpone the larger task. It seems almost necessary at last to make use of that proscribed word, but I shan't do it. I shall avoid it by saying that Loring was awfully good looking, with the sort of features one associates with the Greek heroes. He had hair that barely escaped being black and he brushed it straight back from a high, broad forehead. His eyes were just as dark as his hair, and they always had a sparkle in them. His skin was fairer than that of his companions but it showed plenty of healthy color. In fact, perfect health was perhaps the first thing you thought of in connection with Loring, and perfect health is the one thing he possessed to a lesser extent than any of the three.

Health means bodily soundness, and Loring's body was not sound. Under the light rug which covered him from the waist down was a pair of legs that just couldn't be depended on to perform the ordinary functions of legs. They looked all right, too, except that the muscles were not as well developed as they should have been in a boy of his age. The trouble was in the bones which, instead of building themselves up as bones normally do, had gone in too heavily for lime. In short, Loring's legs suffered from calcification, which is the scientific way of saying that the bones held too much chalk. Different doctors—and Loring's father, who was a very wealthy man, had employed many—had different names for the boy's trouble, names varying in spelling and length but all meaning about the same thing. Loring spent his days in a wheelchair, and, while the physician who at present had him in charge and who once every two or three months journeyed to Freeburg in an eight thousand dollar car spoke hopefully of ultimate betterment or even complete recovery, the probabilities were that Loring would never get beyond crutches. The fact that he had always been as he was now undoubtedly helped him to accept his fate with cheerfulness. Perhaps at night, after the faithful Wattles had finished his careful massaging of the refractory members and the lights were out, Loring may have been visited by dark and rebellious thoughts, but if so, none would have surmised it. To Clif and Tom, as well as to all others who were intimate with him, his good spirits and patience were things to marvel at. Wyndham was proud of Loring Deane. Proud because, as the son of Sanford Deane, one of the country's wealthiest and most prominent citizens, he lent a certain cachet to the school, but prouder because he had so many qualities that boys whole-heartedly admire wherever found; pluck in adversity, cheerfulness, determination to accept no favors based on his disability and, finally, a keen mind.

To obviate the difficulty of stairs Loring had been given a room on the first corridor of East Hall, next to the office of Mr. Clendennin, Head of the Junior School. Because it would have been awkward for him to sit at the table in Dining Hall his meals were served to him in his room by his attendant, the aforementioned Wattles. Save in these two particulars, however, Loring received no favors, nor sought any. In studies he was brilliant, although he spent no more time in preparation than did Tom. He was an ardent football lover and, in fact, an enthusiast on every sort of sport. And as for chess—well, Wattles had finally progressed to a point where he could occasionally win, but when Loring really put his mind on the game he could beat anyone in school. He had even bested "The Turk" recently, and "The Turk," by which impolite name Mr. Way, the mathematics instructor, was known, was an old, old hand at the game!

Having proved at some length, and conclusively in his own opinion, why it was imperative for the nine to give him the position of second baseman, Tom brought his remarks to a triumphant end. Whereupon two things happened almost simultaneously. The gong out in the corridor clanged, giving notice that study hour in assembly hall was imminent, and the door of Loring's room opened and Wattles appeared.

CHAPTER III
CANDIDATES FOR THE NINE

RATHER HARD LUCK FOR you, after listening to prosy descriptions of Clif, Tom and Loring, to have Wattles come on the scene! But Wattles may be disposed of more briefly. Wattles was about thirty, tall, rather lacking in flesh, with pale brown eyes—a sort of parchment brown they were—a long nose and a retiring chin. Wattles was English. That is to say he had been born in England, and, although he had spent the last ten years in this country and no longer owed allegiance to the King, he was still—and always would be—English in everything save the right to vote! Wattles acted as nurse, valet, companion, secretary and in numerous other capacities for Loring. He was so eminently respectable that Tom, when in his society, felt positively raffish. Wattles wore black on all occasions and never appeared without his square-crowned black derby. When he walked to church in the village on Sunday morning he encased his capable hands in dark-gray gloves, carried his prayerbook and hymnal and looked far more sacerdotal than the minister himself. Tom frequently declared that Wattles was "a scream and a bully sort." As to that the reader may judge for himself later.

Wattles' present return was to prepare Loring for study hour, and after the visitors had hurried away to their respective rooms for their books he proceeded methodically to his task. Loring was carefully lifted from the armchair in which he had been seated to the wheelchair. Then Wattles selected the proper books from the table, together with a scratch pad and a fountain pen, and laid them on a shelf that stretched in front of Loring from one arm of the chair to the other. The rug was laid across the boy's knees and lightly tucked into place. After which, with a final glance around, Wattles said: "Right, sir?"

"Right-o," replied Loring, and Wattles laid hold of the handlebar across the back and propelled the chair through the door and along the corridor to where, at the farther end, wide portals gave a glimpse of the big hall. En route Loring said: "Wattles, I wish you'd look around when you go back to the library and see what you can find about baseball. There are probably some books there. Bring what you can, will you?"

"Baseball, Mr. Loring. Right, sir."

"Yes. I suppose you don't know much about that game, do you, Wattles?"

"I am not, Mr. Loring, what you might call well informed on the subject. I have, though, witnessed several contests of professional baseball and observed it closely, and while there are numerous points—"

"I get you. Well, we'll have to send for some books, I guess. You see, Wattles, we're going to play the game this spring."

"We, sir?" asked Wattles with a trace of surprise.

"Oh, well, I mean Clif and Tom. You and I are going to look on, though, and so it's up to us to study the game thoroughly and get so we understand the—the fine points, eh?"

"Undoubtedly," agreed Wattles. "A most interesting pastime, I've no doubt, if one possesses a thorough knowledge of the intricacies."

"Sure! Don't forget those books from the library."

Wattles looked almost pained as he pushed the chair to its customary location at one side of the doorway and retired. Wattles never forgot.

Two days later candidates for the Wyndham School Baseball Team assembled in the gymnasium. While the rest of the school was contained under one roof, with East, Middle and West Halls forming three sides of a quadrangle, the gymnasium, new and well appointed, was set at a little distance behind East Hall, with which it was connected by a covered walk. This afternoon, since it was raining with the dogged persistence of February rains in the Connecticut hills, the roofed passage was much in vogue. Clif and Tom made use of it, as, a little later, did Loring and Wattles. The candidates gathered in the baseball cage on the ground floor, a big, well-lighted inclosure in which almost any feat of the game might be accomplished save the hitting of anything better than a single. Since the furnishings of the cage were meager, consisting as they did of three backless benches along one side, most of the fellows who had responded to the call stood either inside the cage or in the corridor that bordered it, and conversed with such sang froid as their relations with the team warranted. New candidates spoke in low tones, or not at all, while they viewed curiously and sometimes enviously the veterans of last year's nine. Loring didn't arrive until Mr. Connover had made his appearance and was addressing the assembled throng. The partition between cage and corridor was a wall, well-padded on the inner side, to a height of three and a half feet. Above that a strong wire netting continued to the high ceiling. By sitting very erect in his wheelchair and stretching just a little Loring could see over the wall. Having set the chair in an inconspicuous place near one corner of the cage, Wattles removed his black derby, wiped the sweatband with an immaculate handkerchief, returned the hat to his head and the handkerchief to a pocket and set himself to a grave and intent study of the proceedings.

Mr. Connover said nothing particularly new nor inspiring. He dwelt rather strongly on the fact that the candidates were due for a fortnight or so of somewhat drudging drill and suggested that any who wanted to withdraw had best do so before the squad reassembled. "If," proceeded the coach, "I find you here tomorrow I shall expect you to stick for the duration. Last year we were fortunate enough to get outdoors on the twentieth of March. This year it may be later, or earlier. There's no way of telling. But it's safe to say that you've got a good three weeks of indoor work ahead of you, and any of you who can't stomach that had better quit today."

Mr. Connover was not a large man, nor was he particularly impressive in any way as viewed this afternoon. He had donned an old suit of blue serge and a pair of stained white sneakers. "Steve" in charge of a physics class and "Steve" speaking to a bunch of baseball candidates were different persons. With the single exception of "Lovey" McKnight, chemistry instructor, Mr. Connover was the youngest member of the faculty, being twenty-nine. He had coached the baseball teams for two years before this and had turned out at least average good teams. The fact that only one of them had managed to secure the best two out of three games with Wolcott was no reflection on the coach.

"We have arranged a schedule for this spring that is two games longer than last year's," Mr. Connover was saying now. "It's a mighty good schedule, and Manager Longwell and his assistants deserve praise for working it up." There was a faint, repressed cheer, and "Bi" Longwell, hugging a large pad of paper to him on a bench, grinned. "We're down to meet some good teams, fellows, and we've simply got to play real ball right from the start if we're to make a decent showing by the end of the season. Of course, it's the Wolcott series we're after, but we aren't going to throw any games away before we get to the big ones. I'd like to see this spring a Wyndham team that will take three-fourths of its games. We've got twenty-two scheduled. Probably four at least won't be played, because of weather conditions. I want this team to end the season with fourteen victories, and if it doesn't I'm going to be disappointed in it.

"We've got a lot of good material left over from last year to build on, and we've got a fine captain." There was a real cheer this time. "Captain Leland is going to say a few words to you presently, and I want you to give him strict attention. And we've got, I am sure, a fine lot of new material to build with. So there's no reason why we shouldn't get off to a running start and find our stride early. One thing I must caution you about, fellows, and I say this earnestly. Don't think because you're busy with baseball that you can neglect your studies. The surest way to prove to me that you aren't deserving of a position on the team is to let down in class. If you do that you can't be depended on to finish out the season, and there's no use wasting time now on fellows who aren't going to last and who won't be on hand when they're needed most. Now, fellows, Captain Leland."

Leland, already standing, wrapped his hands more tightly in the hem of an old gray sweat-shirt and faced the forty-odd boys while the chorus of "A-a-ay!" died away. He was plainly embarrassed, but "Hurry"—he had been christened Horace—wasn't the sort to allow embarrassment to keep him from doing what he had to do. Nor even to make him hesitate. He began speaking before the shout of recognition and approval had quite ceased, and Loring, listening and watching from beyond the wire screening, lost the first few words.

"—A few things I'd like to tell you about what we intend to do this year. Coach Connover has spoken of the schedule and said that it's good. And it is. But it's hard, too. We've got teams like Toll's and Broadmoor this year to buck against, and they're good. And plenty of hard teams that we've played before: Murray, Hoskins, Horner, Cupples. We're playing two games with Horner, and two with Highland and Freeburg. And maybe only two with Wolcott, if we fight hard!"

That called for applause, and it was forthcoming. Hurry didn't look at first glance like a captain of baseball, or, for that matter, any sort of a captain. He was of medium height, rather thin, with very light-brown hair and a somewhat colorless complexion. Rather a wisp of a chap as athletes go. But a moment's observation corrected first judgment. His steel-blue eyes were keen, his mouth was determined and his countenance as a whole was, save when he smiled that infrequent and oddly crooked smile of his, seriously intent. His movements were abrupt, and when he started away his head always dropped until his chin nearly rested on his chest. Someone had once said that Hurry did that to decrease resistance to the wind! As a matter of fact, he was of the nervous, quick-thinking and quick-acting type, a fellow who went into a thing with, as the expression is, "all four feet," and the lowered head merely indicated that Hurry, having started for some other place, was earnestly concentrating on how to get there as speedily as possible and what to do when he arrived.

"We've got thirteen home games and nine away, and some of the visits are going to keep us busy! But that doesn't matter. I mean it isn't going to matter if we just make up our minds to one thing; to be the best baseball team that ever trained on the Wyndham field. Coach has talked sense about—I mean—well, he always talks sense, of course—" Hurry's one-sided grin appeared momentarily, while the audience laughed—"but he said a mouthful when he spoke about keeping in right with faculty. I've been here three years, fellows, and I've seen teams hurt more than once because some poor prune who should have known better got in wrong at the Office and wasn't there when he was needed. Coach says we don't want fellows with us who won't study and keep their end up in class, and that goes for me, too.

"About this indoor stuff, now. Well, it won't hurt you a bit, and I'd hate to see any of you duck just because there'll be a couple of weeks of calisthenics. You won't have to work any harder than Mr. Babcock makes you work in gym class. And it's necessary, too. I don't want to see any of you fellows quit without getting a fair try-out. Some of you will quit later, because there's only two teams to fill, but you leave that to Coach Connover. He'll tell you quick enough when he's through with you! Well, I guess that's everything," ended Hurry as the audience chuckled in appreciation of the dry jest. "Just stick as long as you're needed, fellows; and do your best for the Team and the School. I know your best will be good enough!"

Somewhat to the surprise of the candidates, Mr. Connover announced that nothing more was required of them that day. "Be sure to give your names to the Manager before you go," he added. "And that means all of you, old or new. Tomorrow we'll meet on the floor at four-thirty."

Returning to West Hall, Tom remarked: "I wonder how Leland and I will get on together around second. You know, Clif, second baseman and shortstop have simply got to work together smoothly, and that guy doesn't look like a fellow who would take kindly to advice."

"From you?" jeered Clif. "I should hope not! Anyway, you and Hurry Leland aren't likely to see much of each other. He's on the first, you know."

"Meaning that I'll only make the second, eh?"

"Meaning you'll be plaguy lucky if you make the bench! Say, I was sort of looking around back there," continued Clif as he followed Tom into Number 34, "and I'll bet there were twenty last year fellows on hand."

"What of it?" asked Tom, plumping himself into a chair.

"What of it? Well, what chance have a couple of dunderheads like you and me got, I'd like to know."

"Dunderhead yourself," responded Tom, unruffled. "Dunderhead, me no dunderhead, young feller. Listen. I'm an experienced ball player. I was even a captain once."

"Who else was on the team?" laughed Clif. "Your old nurse?"

"Well, of course, that was some time ago; when I was a mere lad of twelve. Just the same we weren't so rotten. We had a pitcher who could strike out fellows weighing twenty pounds less than he did!"

"What's weight got to do with it?" asked Clif, puzzled.

"I'm just telling you." Tom chuckled. "We used to call him 'Skel'; short for Skeleton, you know. He was about ten years old, I guess, and when he came on the field you couldn't tell for sure whether he was walking forwards or backwards. He was the same all round. And round is just the word, too!"

"And what did you play on the 'Morristown Giants'?"

"Wrong. We were the 'Red Sox.' I played catcher sometimes, and sometimes I played third base and sometimes—"

"You picked up bats. I know. Well, all that's mighty interesting, Tom, but I can't just see it helping you much in the present crisis. Of course you might tell it to Steve, but he's sort of hard-boiled and—"

"No, sir," interrupted Tom determinedly, "I won't attempt to influence him. I propose to win the honor of playing second base by working up from the ranks, like the rest of you."

"Very high-minded," said Clif approvingly. "And, speaking of ranks, I'll bet you'll be ranker than any."

"Say, joking aside, Clif, we *have* got rather a cheek to try for that team and hope to get anywhere. I didn't see more than five or six other third class fellows there."

"Glad you acknowledge it. Still, it isn't going to do us any harm to make a stab at it. We might cop something. You, anyway. You've played more than I have."

"Well, heck, nothing venture, you know. Cheer up, old timer. You never can tell. One of us may be saving the day yet with a timely clout. Speaking of timely clouts, when I captained the old Red Sox—"

"Brakes!" said Clif rudely.

CHAPTER IV
MR. BINGHAM ENTERTAINS

WELL, THAT FIRST FORTNIGHT of work for the baseball candidates *was* a good deal like drudgery. As Tom said, it wasn't so hard, but it was blamed monotonous. Led by Coach Connover, or sometimes by Captain Leland, they went through a daily program of calisthenics that seemed designed to acquaint them with the possession of muscles they had never before even suspected. The ordinary setting-up exercises, amended to suit the coach's notions, began the session. After that they swung clubs—at first in imminent danger from each other—and went through strange exercises with dumbbells, the latter to limber up wrist and forearm muscles. Toward the latter part of the fortnight the day's program ended with instructions on holding and swinging the bat, but it was not until the beginning of the third week that they abandoned the gymnasium floor and moved into the cage.

There were then forty-six candidates; not so many for a school which held that term one hundred and eighty-four students. Still, as some eighty of the latter number were either Junior School pupils or members of the fourth class, and in both cases ineligible for school teams, perhaps the showing wasn't so bad, after all. Of the forty-six, eleven had played with last season's first team at one time or another, although only five had taken part in the Wolcott series, and seven more had been second team members. Most of the rest had had more or less experience playing scrub baseball or, like Clif and Tom, were newcomers at Wyndham. A number had won fame in other sports, for the squad included nearly a dozen football players, several of the recently disbanded basketball team, several track men and three fellows who had aided in the defeat of Wolcott on the ice. The latter were, besides Clif, Raiford and Coles. In spite of the monotony, those drills usually provided some amusement before they were over, and, on the whole, it was all pretty good fun.

Encouragingly, winter withdrew over the blue hills to the north during the first week of March, and, while it took many mild days to thaw the ground out, by the middle of the month word came that, barring more rain or snow, the baseball candidates could count on getting out of doors by the nineteenth.

That announcement was cheering, for, although in lieu of the diamond the cage provided a fine practice space, everyone longed to feel the spring of the turf under his feet and the wind in his face. It was evident that the latter longing was due to be satisfied, for no windier March ever visited Freeburg than this one. But, since neither rain nor snow intervened before the anxiously awaited Wednesday, the wind proved a friend rather than a foe, ably aiding the sun to dry the already greening sod of the field. And on Wednesday, in the face of a tearing westerly gale, but under the bluest of blue skies, the Wyndham baseball squad romped out of the locker room and across to the practice diamond as gayly as a lot of colts turned out to pasture.

I would like to be able to narrate that Clif and Tom had applied themselves so diligently to the work in hand and showed such aptitude for baseball that they were now marked members of the squad. But I can't. Their diligence had been—well, let us say normal. At times it had been plainly in evidence; at other times it had waned. Indoor practice doesn't arouse enthusiasm, as a rule, after the novelty has worn off. In short, when the squad went out to the field that Wednesday afternoon Clif and Tom were just two possibilities amongst two score.

The coach didn't seem to take practice very seriously today. A number of balls were given out and for twenty minutes or so these were tossed about from one player to another, usually for a distance of no more than twenty feet. A simple, easy appearing pastime, this, but one which nevertheless, if correctly indulged in, called nearly every muscle of the body into play and speedily warmed one up to the point of perspiration—or beyond. In tossing as a preliminary to real work, the ball, as Clif soon discovered, was not delivered you where you could reach it the easiest but where you had to exert yourself to get it; at one side, overhead, shoe-high; in brief, anywhere save where you might reasonably expect it. Having caught it—or missed it—your play was to snap it back as soon as possible in the general direction of the next catcher; and the more general the direction the better. For awhile this sort of thing seems real fun, and there is much laughter, much shouting and many gymnastic performances, but after, say, ten minutes the laughter subsides, suppressed groans succeed the shouts and extraordinary attempts to capture the ball become fewer and fewer. And by this time your body is in a healthy glow, you are probably perspiring from every pore and you wish to goodness that Coach would think up a new stunt!

And presently he did. The candidates for pitcher went off by themselves; Jeff Ogden, last season's ace, Bud Moore, Erlingby, Frost. With them went two others to catch their easy offerings. Manager Longwell hit slow bunts to a selected few. For the rest there was labor on the diamond or at the plate. With five men playing infield and six sharing the further territory, with Pat Tyson in the box and Assistant Manager Cotter behind him to feed the balls to him, the remaining candidates took turns with the bat. They were warned against slugging the ball, and it was infrequent that it went beyond the infield. Long or fast throws were prohibited by the fielders and more than once a too-energetic or too-ambitious player was reprimanded. The outfielders caught or chased flies sent up by Gus Risley, but they were not allowed to return the ball all the way to him in the air, and when one committed that breach of the law he was fiercely called to order by Jimmy Cunningham, catching for Gus. Jimmy was Second Assistant Manager and fully aware of the dignity and authority connected with his position. Frequent changes were made, and in the course of a half-hour everyone made the journey to the plate twice. When practice ended, which it did very early, there were many tired youths among those who, obeying instructions, trotted all the way back to the gymnasium; and, despite that preliminary work indoors, there were many, many sore muscles.

By Saturday outdoor conditions were better. The turf lost its sogginess, the base paths hardened and a chill wind no longer endangered overheated bodies. By Saturday, too, most of the restrictions had been removed and practice looked more like the genuine article. There was even a three-inning game that afternoon between the newly formed first and second squads, and, while no score was kept, there was plenty of hard playing. Tod Raiford, outfield candidate playing with the first squad, landed against one of Frost's straight ones and hit it almost to the center of the football field for four bases. To be sure, second-squad members protested loudly that it had fallen foul, but since the foul-line flags had not yet been put into place they couldn't prove it and Tod was given the benefit of the doubt. "Bi" Longwell, officiating as umpire from behind the pitcher, gravely proclaimed it fair, although since he had not left his position to judge its flight there were those impolite enough to say that he didn't know anything about it. Cooper, catching for the second squad, good-naturedly offered to settle the question after practice, with or without gloves, but Bi threatened to fine him and Cooper subsided.

Clif and Tom were allowed a few minutes of participation in that brief contest, but their appearance with the second, Clif in left field and Tom on third base, could not truthfully be said to add perceptible strength to the team. Of the two only Tom went to bat, and the best he could do was pop an easy foul to Catcher Cobham. Clif failed to distinguish himself by even that much, since the first team batsmen thoughtlessly failed to hit the ball anywhere near his position. Nevertheless both boys ended that week with increased ambition and enthusiasm. Also, it must be added, with decreased expectations of winning renown on the diamond. There was no doubt but that, viewed without prejudice, they were pretty small fry in the baseball sea. Tom pretended, however, to believe that as the season progressed those in command would discover his now concealed talent and install him at some post of honor on the big team, preferably second base. Clif, on the other hand, might easily have lost courage about that time and modestly withdrawn from competition had it not been for Tom and Loring. Tom's argument was that you never could tell what was going to happen and that an epidemic or an earthquake or something equally devastating might any day wipe out a couple of handfulls of Clif's rivals. "Then," added Tom reasonably enough, "you'd be mighty sorry you didn't stick!" Loring's argument was that it would be the part of wisdom to stay with the squad just as long as he was allowed to stay and learn all he could so that next year, if not this, he would be all set to accept the captaincy or any other little job that might be lying around! Perhaps Clif's own inclinations weighed more than advice, though, for, although he was frequently discouraged by his own ineptitude and certain that he wouldn't survive the final cut in the squad, he had always believed in finishing what he started. Not a bad belief to hold, that, for persistence has often won where courage has failed.

Clif's father made one of his frequent visits to school the following Sunday. Clif's mother was dead, and he was the only child. In consequence he and his father had been pretty close for many years, and, until weather conditions had prevented during late January and early February, Mr. Bingham had averaged two trips a month from Providence by automobile. The present visit was the first for over three weeks, and Clif forgot the self-consciousness that was likely to assail him at such times and squeezed his father's hand so hard that Mr. Bingham flinched perceptibly. He rolled up to the Inn shortly before church time, the blue car well spattered with mud, and Clif didn't have much time for conversation then. A few questions and replies, an appointment for dinner at one—to be kept, however, as soon as church was over, and accompanied by Tom—and Clif had to hurry back to school. As the Freeburg Inn was only a block from the school entrance he was able to make the journey in three minutes flat.

Usually Clif made up a quartet for dinner at the Inn by inviting two of his friends, generally Tom and Walter Treat. Walter was Clif's roommate in Number 17 West Hall, a quiet, studious, rather self-contained youth of seventeen. Clif liked him thoroughly, although not so well as Tom, and Clif's father had long since fallen victim to his attractions, the greatest of which, in Mr. Bingham's judgment, being an ability to converse intelligently on subjects other than school athletics. Today, however, as frequently happened,

Walter's own folks were visiting school, and while Clif would have liked to have had Loring to dinner in Walter's place, Loring wouldn't be persuaded. Not generally sensitive about his condition, Loring disliked displaying his infirmity in public dining rooms. So when at a few minutes past one Mr. Bingham's party seated itself at table it consisted only of the host, Tom and Clif. Whatever was to be said of the Inn's Sunday dinners—and much that was complimentary might have been said—they could not be criticized on the score of astounding originality. You always knew just what to expect. Today's dish of olives and pickles looked exactly like last Sunday's, the cream of tomato with rice tasted exactly like the soup of a week ago, and so it went right down the menu, through the fish and the broiled milk-fed chicken and the three vegetables and the combination salad and the harlequin ice-cream to the demi-tasse and the far too pliable crackers, which, aided by a square of yellow cheese, ended the banquet. But it was good, that dinner, and especially toothsome to fellows who for nearly a month had subsisted on a possibly more appropriate but far plainer diet. Tom, as always, lost no time in approaching the task at hand, nor wasted strength on conversation. Where dining was concerned Tom's was a one-track mind!

Clif and his father, however, found leisure for talking; leisure, too, to regard the other occupants of the big, sunny room and to exchange bows with a few of them. At a near-by table Walter Treat, his father and mother and a kid brother were dining. Several others of Clif's acquaintances were also on hand, while, over by an open window, a thin, somewhat sallow-looking man who ate alone glanced up and nodded as he encountered Mr. Bingham's eyes. "Rather an interesting chap I ran into this morning," said Mr. Bingham, responding to Clif's mute inquiry. "Cooper, I think his name is."

"There's a Cooper on the scrub team," answered Clif. "Jack Cooper. Maybe his father. Doesn't look like Jack much, though."

"Probably is, however. At least, I gathered that he's staying at the Inn more or less permanently. For that matter, son, you don't look an awful lot like your dad."

"I don't suppose I do," said Clif. "I favor mother more, don't I?"

Mr. Bingham nodded, thoughtfully studying his son's face. Tom, supposedly deaf, burst into speech. "Heck, Clif, you and your father are dead ringers, only you'll never be as good looking as he is."

Mr. Bingham laughed. "Thanks, Tom," he said. "I appreciate that even though I recognize it as rank flattery. When you reach forty you become grateful for any kind word."

"'S all right," replied Tom stoutly. "I know what I'm talking about. When we came in here all the girls, and the old dames, too, began to sit up and take notice, and I'll bet it wasn't Clif that made 'em do it, nor me either!"

Well, Mr. Bingham *was* a fine-looking man, and if he was forty—or nearly forty—you'd never have suspected it. Clif was very proud of his father, and Tom's compliment, even if a bit crude, pleased him. Looking about the room he saw that Mr. Cooper's gaze was directed toward their table. The gaze was courteously but unhurriedly withdrawn the next instant, and Clif tried to discover a resemblance between the lean, pleasantly grave countenance and the round, freckled face of the second nine catcher, and failed. Probably Jack Cooper, too, took after his mother, he reflected.

After dinner, while Mr. Bingham smoked a short cigar on the porch before taking his guests to ride, Walter Treat brought his father and mother up and there were introductions all around. When they had presently departed Mr. Bingham looked about searchingly. "Wonder where that Cooper chap is," he said. "Told him I'd like to have him meet you, son, and he seemed quite anxious to. But he doesn't appear to be about."

"Maybe," responded Clif, "he will be around when we get back, dad." He was far more concerned with the approaching automobile ride than with meeting strangers, no matter how interesting the latter might seem to his father. Tom, tilted back in a porch chair, was somnolent, but Clif watched his father's cigar and reflected that he had never seen one which diminished more slowly. Eventually, though, Mr. Bingham arose with a sigh and dropped the cigar over the railing.

"Well, boys, let's go," he said. "What part of the world do you want to see today?"

It was after four when they returned to the Inn. The elusive Mr. Cooper was not in sight, and presently Mr. Bingham said good-by and sped away, the boys waving him out of sight before turning their steps toward school. With a long sigh for the departed glories of the day, Tom thrust an inquiring finger under his belt, "That was a great feed, Clif," he murmured.

CHAPTER V
TOM CONFIDES

AFTER THAT, WHILE THEY walked up the curving drive, between rows of leafless trees, Tom was unusually silent. Nearing West Hall, Clif suggested continuing on and paying a call on Loring, but Tom shook his head. "Let's go up to your room," he said.

Number 17 looked out on the court formed by the old building, known as Middle Hall, and the two wings, East and West, and even at midday was none too well lighted. Now, at half-past four, it was decidedly gloomy, and Clif would have turned on the light had not Tom protested. "Lights hurt a fellow's eyes," he said. "Besides, I like twilight, anyway."

"Sounds so," said Clif. "You're as cheerful as an undertaker!" Walter was still absent and the window-seat and the floor beside it were littered with Sunday newspapers. Tom swept them from the cushion and stretched himself out and Clif drew up a chair so that he might rest his feet beside Tom's. Across the court, the wall of East Hall was in purple shadow. On the slates of the roof three pigeons walked pompously to and fro, cooing softly, while below, in the shrubbery, sparrows chirped in noisy argument.

"Fathers," observed Tom after a moment, "are a great institution, aren't they?"

"Yes, I suppose so," answered Clif. "But how do you mean?"

Tom didn't elucidate. Instead: "Say, remember how mad you were with me the day you came?" he asked. "You were saying good-by to your father down there at the car and I was sitting on the steps. Remember? You wanted to fight."

"Why not?" inquired Clif warmly. "You sat there, grinning like a Hindoo idol, and told me to go and have a cry and I'd feel better. Of course I wanted to fight!"

"Sure," said Tom soberly. "I don't blame you. I did act sort of rotten."

"You sure did," agreed Clif, but without animus. "And I certainly did dislike you a lot. But, of course, you were funking a date with Alick, who was going to tell you whether you were to beat it back home or stick around awhile—"

"Yes, but that wasn't the reason I was nasty," interrupted Tom. "I said, that night in recreation room, that maybe I'd tell you about it some time, and I guess I'd like to do it now. I feel sort of melancholy and—and confiding. Maybe I've got a touch of indigestion. Or maybe it's the effect of the twilight."

"Let's light up and forget it," offered Clif cheerfully.

"No, I want to talk. Listen, Clif. The real reason I was nasty that time was because I was—was—heck, I don't know just how to put it. Guess I was sort of jealous."

"Jealous!" echoed Clif.

"Well, envious then. I could see what corking pals you and your dad were, and what a lot you thought of each other and how you were both kind of choked up about saying good-by, and it made me feel like the dickens. You see, I never had any father, Clif."

"Never had—" gasped Clif.

"None that I can remember," said Tom gloomily. "He—went away when I was five years old."

"Oh," murmured Clif. "I wondered. You never spoke of him, although you did tell me that your mother was dead and that you had a guardian."

"Mother died when I was about ten. From what I can make out we're a queer lot, us Kembles. As far as I know I haven't a relation living, and about all I've learned of the family is what old Winslow has told me; and he's not much of a talker. He's a lawyer; one of the sort who hates to say anything unless you pay 'im a fee first. But I do know that my mother was born in this country and my father in England. He met her over here and they were married. He had something to do with cotton; represented an English firm and traveled around for them. Mother traveled with him. I was born in Mobile, Alabama. Then, five years later, my dad up and beat it. Of course I don't know the rights of it, Clif. Mother never spoke of him more than a couple of times that I can remember, and Winslow didn't know him. I suppose he was a rotter. Still—"

Tom relapsed into silence. Then, after a moment or two he went on. "I was pretty fond of my mother, Clif, although I was only a kid when she died, but when I look back and remember things it seems to me that perhaps it wasn't all his fault; my father's I mean. A fellow hates like the dickens to say anything against his mother, and—well, I'm not going to. She was always a corker to me. But what I mean is—well, father might have found her trying. Heck, I don't know! I ought to hate him, and sometimes I do, but maybe he had some excuse for lighting out."

"He never came back?" asked Clif.

"No. I don't know whether mother ever heard from him again, but Winslow says he provided decently for her and me. Put some money in a bank, you know, and mother received so much every month. She was sort of extravagant, though, I guess, because a couple of years before she died she tried to get hold of the—whatyoucallit—principal. That's when old Winslow came into it. She got him to try to get the money for her. He didn't succeed, but he kept on trying, and he was still at it when mother died. That's how she came to make him my guardian. She thought he was the eel's whiskers."

"I've heard," said Clif when Tom had been silent a space, "that the English are great folks for traveling about. Englishmen especially. Maybe your father was like that, Tom. Wasn't contented to stay put, you know."

"I'm pretty sure of it," answered Tom. "I'm that way myself, worse luck. I can't hear a train whistle or a steamship toot without getting a thrill, I can be happy for hours looking at a map and I never see a road that I don't feel my feet itching to find out what's at the end of it. Ever feel that way? Well, I guess I get all that from my father. Oh, I could forgive him for leaving my mother, because, as I've told you, there might have been some excuse, but what I can't forgive him is not showing up or sending some word after she died. You'd think he might be at least faintly interested in me, Clif. That's what I've got in for him, and I'd like mighty well to see him some day just long enough to tell him what I think of him!"

"But, Tom, doesn't it seem probable that—that he's dead? It's—how long?—eleven years, isn't it, since he went off?"

"Yes, he may be dead. I suppose he is. That is, sometimes I do, and other times I'm plumb certain he isn't. Winslow wanted to spend a lot of money and find out about him; who he was and what had become of him; but I wouldn't let him. Told him if he did he'd have to spend his own money. He wasn't keen for that. Oh, I don't really care now. I've got along without a father for nearly twelve years and I guess I can keep on. Only—only sometimes—when I see other fellows with theirs—"

Tom relapsed into silence. Clif, searching for words that would express the sympathy he felt without offending the other's pride, said nothing. Presently Tom broke the silence with: "Well, that's that. Sorry to have bored you, old scout, but I rather wanted you to know the real reason why I acted so like a bounder that day. I've wanted to tell you ever since, but a fellow sort of hesitates to talk about his private affairs."

"I'm very glad you did tell me," answered Clif through the dusk. He wanted to say more, but again the right words eluded him. After a moment or two Tom swung his feet to the floor with a bang.

"Heck, let's have some light," he exclaimed. "This is enough to give a fellow the willies!"

On Tuesday the second team came into official existence, and Mr. Wadleigh took charge as coach. Mr. Wadleigh lived in Greenville, some twenty miles distant, and made the daily pilgrimage to Freeburg in a dilapidated Ford car whose mudguards were so loose that they flapped up and down like wings and gave the battered vehicle the appearance of flying. As Mr. Wadleigh seldom drove under thirty-five miles an hour—his record between the two villages was alleged to be thirty-two minutes—the illusion was enhanced. Many years before he had played baseball on the Wyndham team. No one could discover that he had distinguished himself, however. He was in business of some sort in Greenville—real estate, rumor had it, and for several years past had donated his services to his old school, doubtless at some sacrifice. He was a tall, awkward-looking man of perhaps thirty-three or -four years with a very prominent nose set in a long face. He was rather bald, a fact especially noticeable because he was never seen wearing a hat. Some held that the hair had been blown from the front and top of his head by the wind during his wild, careening flights over the road. He constantly wore an amiable smile which exposed a number of long teeth below a ragged mustache of a faded brown. That smile, however, was not to be taken—no pun is intended—at its face value. It persisted even when "Tusks" was not pleased with things. The nickname implied no disrespect, for, while Mr. Wadleigh was not beautiful to look upon, nor possessed graces of manner, he was, in school parlance, "a wow of a coach."

Tusks took over twenty-four candidates from Coach Connover, conducted them to the second-team diamond, looked them over in thoughtful, if smiling, silence and set them to work. Three days later, still smiling amiably, he dismissed seven of the twenty-four. Through some, to them, inexplicable miracle, Clif and Tom survived the cut. The next day, Saturday, the second shortened practice and watched the first play six innings of its game with the local High School nine. The day was a miserable one from a baseball viewpoint, with cloudy skies and a brisk north wind, a day far too chill to permit of good playing had either of the contesting teams been capable of it, which they apparently were not. The five pitchers, of which three wore the dark blue of Wyndham, were hit hard at all times, and hits coupled with numerous errors and many misplays which didn't appear in the error column fattened the score of each side. The bulk of the audience survived the last of the seventh inning, by which time the home team had a five-run lead, but after that it disintegrated rapidly. When, in the first half of the ninth, High School staged a rally only a corporal's guard of devoted adherents remained in the stand to witness it.

Erlingby, who had taken Ogden's place in the box for Wyndham at the beginning of the eighth inning, started out with a pass to the visitor's third baseman. He followed that with a wild throw in an effort to catch the runner off the bag, and the High School player went all the way to third. That worried Erlingby and heartened the visitors. The next man up laid a slow bunt down on the first base line and Erlingby handled it. The man on third faked a dash to the plate, delaying the pitcher just long enough to make his hurried throw to Van Dyke, at first, too late. The High School left fielder hit to short right and scored the first runner, the latter beating Coles' shot to the plate by an eyelash. A pinch hitter batted for the next on the list and cracked the first ball pitched into deep left. Talbott made a pretty running catch, but another run tallied. The enemy's catcher fouled off four balls before he straightened one out right across second base. That brought in the third score of the inning. In trying to reach second on Greene's peg to the rubber, however, the Freeburg catcher was caught a yard off the cushion, and, with two down and the pitcher up, Wyndham breathed with relief. A second pinch hitter took the pitcher's place, though, and several bad moments ensued. Erlingby failed twice to cut the corners and then scored a strike on a long foul down the left base-line. Another ball, and then a fast one across the platter and a second foul-strike. A third foul, back of the plate, just escaped Cobham's glove. Then the batsman crashed against the next delivery and drove it high and far into left field. Once again Sid Talbott won applause from the remaining handful of spectators, this time by sprinting far to his right and getting under the ball just as it came to earth, foul by more than a yard.

That ended the rally and the game, giving Wyndham the contest, 13 to 11.

The following Monday the second team faced the first and wallowed through five innings of horrible baseball. Mr. Wadleigh smiled through it all, but none of his charges labored under the mistaken assumption that his smile denoted approval. About every second nine player made at least one error that afternoon. Burden, playing third base through three of the chapters, made four! Jones, who succeeded him, did a little better, although he managed to make himself accountable for one of the nine runs accumulated by the enemy. The one thing that kept the first from piling up twice nine runs was their inability to run bases. They had no difficulty in hitting Frost and Purdy, but, once on first, they didn't seem to know what to do. Purdy caught runners off five times, and in the fourth inning Leland and Raiford couldn't decide which of them was entitled to possession of second base, and pending a decision Carr tagged them both and then, to make certain, threw to third. Twice, too, headless running spelled disaster for the first, once when Al Greene sought to score from third on a bunt to pitcher and once when Pat Tyson, a slow runner, tried to stretch his single into a double and was caught ten feet from second.

Neither of the second team's pitchers showed anything that day but willingness. Frost, a left-hander, went well for one inning and then became wild, allowing four hits, passing one man and landing the sphere against Cobham's ribs. Purdy, who took over the job with two on bases, retired the side without further damage, but Billy only possessed a couple of good curves and a slow ball and after the first team batters got acquainted with him in the fourth inning he was hit hard.

Tusks tried out most of his talent before the fifth inning was over, and both Clif and Tom saw service. Tom played second base for half an inning and Clif center field. Tom made a good stop of a hard bounder and then fumbled it long enough to let the runner reach first safely. Clif had no chances. Neither of the two reached the plate with a bat. Afterwards, in the gymnasium, Mr. Wadleigh astounded all hands by smilingly remarking that although they needed practice they had the making of a fine team. At first they suspected him of bitter sarcasm, but later they agreed that he had meant just what he had said, and they hoped hard that he was right!

CHAPTER VI
PSYCHOLOGY

BY WEDNESDAY THE SECOND—OR the "Tuskers," as the first surreptitiously called it—was doing rather better. Neither Frost nor Purdy yet had anything much to offer, and they yielded hits continuously, but the infield pulled itself together and here and there an individual shone brightly. "Slim" Scott, at first base, for instance, began to show rather a talent for his work. Slim was tall and long of arm, and, while somewhat deliberate, was also dependably steady. Connell, shortstop, who had recently been chosen captain, was another high spot. And then there was Jack Cooper, first choice catcher, hard-working and plucky, who handled the pitchers nicely and could peg a good throw to second. As for the others, they were so far no more than promises, and as for batting, well, the second hadn't yet discovered just what that was, but it was learning. Tusks put the team through a solid hour of practice every afternoon before he led it across to oppose the first, and batting in front of the net consumed the major portion of the period. Clif began to show promise as a hitter, although there were plenty who bettered him at it daily, while Tom, with more playing experience, was making slow progress. Perhaps this was partly because Tom had much to unlearn. Tusks had ideas of his own on batting form and was quite out of sympathy with individual eccentricities. A few of the second-nine candidates who had undergone instruction at his hands before got along very well during that first fortnight, but the rest were continually being reminded to stand up to the plate, which, with Billy Purdy in one of his erratic moods, was something requiring real physical courage. Nevertheless, Tusks required that the batters should fairly toe the rubber. "If you can't get out of the way of a ball before it hits you," he said, "you're too slow to bat at all."

He was also down on "swings." If you wanted to please Tusks you held the bat a foot from the end and never, never let it get behind your shoulder. Many of the fellows had their own particular idols and tried to copy their styles; there were at least half a dozen imaginary Ruths in the second squad, but this course was speedily discouraged by the coach. "After you're playing ball for half a dozen years," he said one day to Evans, "you can stand any way you like and swing any way you like, and walk to first on your hands, if you fancy doing it, but there's only one way to learn to bat, and that way's the *right* way. And when you fellows spread your feet all over the box or start your swing from somewhere around the back of your necks you're all wrong. If I want to hit a nail on the head with a hammer I don't hold the hammer off at arm's length. I hold it a foot or so away, and when I strike I hit the nail and not my thumb. In other words, fellows, the longer the swing the less accuracy. Now try it again, Evans. Shorten your grip. That's better. Now, watch the ball and meet it square."

One of Mr. Wadleigh's favorite slogans was "Hit with your eyes!" Elaborated, that meant that you were to watch the pitcher from the instant you stepped into the box until the ball left his hand. After that you were to watch the ball. "Sometimes you can learn by watching the pitcher what sort of a ball he's going to offer you. Very few pitchers that you'll face can throw a curve with the same motion they throw a straight ball. Learn to note the difference. Study the pitcher, even when you're on the bench. When he pitches glue your eyes to the ball and watch it until you've hit it or it's gone by you. You'll learn after a while to detect the wide ones and let them alone. The trouble with most of you right now is that you're afraid to have a strike called on you, and you go after the ball no matter where it is. Remember that it's only the third strike that carries a sting. That's the one you must be ready for. It's only weak batters who worry when the count's against them. The experienced batters realize that if the pitcher has pinned two strikes on them the law of average is against his getting a third one over. Learn to let the 'teasers' alone and concentrate on the good ones. Hit with your eyes!"

Clif, having played but little ball before this spring, had fewer mistakes to correct than many of the others and followed Tusks' instructions without questioning them. He began by standing up to the plate, keeping his feet together—the coach wasn't insistent on that, but advised it—and confining his efforts to hitting the ball at no more than a half swing. Of course he developed faults, such as pulling away as he struck, but they were corrected before they had time to become habits. Tom, on the other hand, was prone to crouch as the ball sped toward him and straighten up as he swung, and, for this reason or some other, invariably hit, when he did hit, into the air. He was willing enough to substitute the coach's methods for his own, but he found difficulty in doing it.

There was much discussion between Tom and Clif—yes, and Loring, too—on the subject of batting. Tom invariably instanced the phenomenal hitting of one "Clouter" Hearn, who played on one of the New Jersey State League teams, when either of the other members of the Triumvirate tactfully questioned the efficacy of his style. Clouter, it appeared, had never batted for less than .368, and Tom's form was molded closely on Clouter's. "Of course," he said one evening in Loring's room, "I don't say that Tusks doesn't know his business or that his dope isn't right, but just the same I believe I can get a heap better results batting my own way than his. I could most always get a couple of good whangs off Purdy when I was doing the way I'm used to doing, but now, since I've been standing like a wooden soldier and sort of pecking at the ball, I don't do a blame thing but fan!"

"I noticed, though," remarked Loring, "that you generally hit flies, Tom."

"Well, I hit! And that's more than I can do now."

"You'll get onto it," soothed Clif. "It takes time."

"Just the same, I still think Tusks ought to let us hit the way it's easiest for us to hit," said Tom doggedly. "After all, it's results that count, isn't it? Sure! Well, then!"

"Probably Mr. Wadleigh thinks the results will be better when you thoroughly learn his way of batting," said Loring. "I notice that men like Baker and Cobb hit about the way Mr. Wadleigh is teaching."

"Back numbers!" snorted Tom. "Now this guy Clouter Hearn—"

"All right," agreed Loring imperturbably, "let's take some who aren't. Sisler or Speaker, for example—"

"But, heck, I don't know how those fellows bat," protested Tom, "and you don't either. You say—"

"But I do know," answered Loring, smilingly. "I never saw them play, but I've got pictures of them at bat."

"Pictures!" grumbled Tom. "Well, I guess I could find plenty of guys who hit over three hundred and don't do it the way Tusks wants us to. I say every man for himself when it comes to hitting the old pill. It's hits that count, no matter whether you get 'em standing on your two feet or on your left ear, by heck!"

"Right," laughed Loring, "but the trouble is, Tom, that you can't get them standing on your left ear, nor your right ear. As I understand it, and I've been out to most every practice, as you know, Tusks has to teach one method to all you fellows alike, and he's teaching the one he considers to be the best. Isn't that the way you understand it?"

"The weak point about Tusks," remarked Clif regretfully, "is that he never saw Clouter Hearn play!"

"Shut up," said Tom, grinning. "Oh, I don't say Tusks isn't all right, Loring. And I suppose he does have to teach one style to the lot of us. And I'm willing enough to bat the way he says, even if I still think I can do better batting my own way, but, Sacred Ibis of the River Nile, fellows, I can't get the hang of his way! I start all right and then Purdy or Frosty gets my goat and I forget all about acting pretty and Tusks is on my neck again. But, heck, what's the use of worrying about it, anyway? I've got as much chance of making the big team as a pig has to fly. Why should I lose weight over my batting?"

"What's the matter," asked Clif mildly, "with playing on the second? We can't all be heroes, you know. I wouldn't be surprised if we got a lot of fun out of it, Tom. Besides, as Mr. Babcock told us last fall when we were on the scrub eleven, it's the lowly second team that teaches the first how to play! He also serves, you know, who only sits and—"

"Plays the goat," aided Tom. "Well, that's all right, too, but it doesn't look to me as if I'd even get a place on the second. Tusks will only keep, maybe, a dozen fellows, besides the pitchers, and I saw him looking at me just this afternoon in a way I didn't like at all. He had a sort of 'Fe fi, fo, fum' expression! I'll bet the next time there's a decrease in the squad, I'll be one of the decreasees!"

"No, you won't," said Loring confidently, "and I'll tell you why. I've been watching, Tom, and I know for a fact that there are at least four other fellows on the squad now who play considerably worse than you do."

"Of which I'm one," said Clif sadly.

"No, you're not. I could tell you their names, but I'm not going to. Mr. Wadleigh has cut the squad to seventeen already, fellows, and he can't drop more than three more."

"Oh, yes, he can," contradicted Tom. "Because Steve will be letting four or five go pretty quick, and they'll drop back into our gang."

"Well, even so," Loring replied, "I still think your chance of staying is good, Tom. And Clif's, too. And, what's more, I want you to stay, both of you. I'm getting interested in baseball, and I want someone I know to watch. I can't play myself, but I can follow your fortunes and feel almost as if I were. And now here's where the Triumvirate gets busy and does its stuff. There are three of us, and there's only one Mr. Wadleigh, and if we can't convince him, between us, that you and Clif are necessary to the team, why, we—we're a punk Triumvirate!"

"Sounds fair enough," said Tom, "but just how are we going to do it?"

"Well, I don't quite know—yet," confessed Loring, "but I believe there's a way. Do you know anything about psychology?"

"Not much. I had one a couple of years ago, but I ran it against an ice-wagon."

"Cut out the comedy," said Clif severely. "Loring's got a scheme. Let's hear it."

"Well, I suppose it is just an idea so far. But here's the way it looks to me, Clif. Suppose you and Tom make up your minds firmly to play good ball and make the second. And suppose I make up my mind just as earnestly to do everything I can to help you. That makes three of us, all—all concentrating on one purpose, one result, doesn't it?"

"Your arithmetic is perfect," said Tom gravely.

"Well, there must be something in this psychology stuff," continued Loring. "I mean in the mastery of the will and—and mental suggestion and all that. You read of all sorts of cases where the thing's been done. Some of them must be true, don't you think?"

"You mean," asked Clif, "that we are to will ourselves onto the second team?"

"Not exactly that. I mean you are to start right now with the determination to make the team and work as hard as you know how; make up your minds to play better every day—"

"Every day in every play I'm getting—"

"Shut up, Tom!" said Clif. "While we're trying to make the team we're to keep telling ourselves that we're *going* to. Is that it, Loring?"

"Yes. Suppose the fellows who are after the positions you want play hard but don't keep their minds on what they're after, don't use their wills; and suppose you play just as hard and never lose sight of why you're doing it, of what you're going after, and use all your will power. Isn't it fair to assume that you'll have the edge on the other chaps?"

"Y-yes," assented Clif. "I see what you mean."

"So do I," said Tom, "but what I'd like to know is what's to prevent those other guys trying the psychology stunt too!"

"Nothing, but they just won't think of it. You hadn't, had you?"

"I'll say I hadn't! Heck, I never took much stock in this mental suggestion stuff, Loring. It always sounds nutty to me."

"I don't think it's nutty," said Loring. "Doesn't it stand to reason that your chance of getting a thing is better if you bend all your energies to getting it? And a fellow's energies aren't wholly physical, are they? His mind—"

"That's all right, but this thing of 'willing' something to happen, now; that's different from just *wanting* it to, isn't it?"

"Yes, it is. You can want anything a whole lot and yet not set your mental energies to the job of going after it. That's the point I'm trying to make. Look here, Tom, have you ever watched a pole-vaulter at work? Do you suppose that he's thinking about what he's going to have for supper or—or some fool thing like that? He isn't. He's saying to himself, *hard*: 'I'm going to do it! I'm going over! This time I'm going to *make* it!' And he isn't thinking about a thing in the world but just getting up there and straightening his body out right and clearing that bar! And if he didn't *think* he was going to do it, if he didn't use his will as well as his body, he never would do it!"

"Keno!" said Tom. "I get you, old scout. Like when Clif made that last goal in the hockey game awhile back. I'll bet it was just his *will* that shot that puck in, for, goodness knows, he didn't have any command over the rest of him!"

Clif laughed, but Loring went on, still seriously. "'Work and Will' is the slogan, fellows. But we don't have to stop there. Remember that it's 'one for all and all for one.' Each of us helps the others every chance he gets."

"Such as how?" asked Clif.

"Well, if you see Tom doing something the wrong way you'll tell him. If Tom sees you making mistakes he will tell you. If I see either of you missing an opportunity I'll put my oar in. Being on the side-lines, so to speak, I might, you know. Then there's propaganda. Whenever any of us sees a chance to speak a good word for another we'll do it. And there may be other ways, too. The main thing is to be looking for them and to use them. Now what do you say? Remember it's three to one, and that's a sure thing in any fight!"

"Looks to me," objected Tom, "more like three to two. Suppose I want to play second base. I've got 'Stu' Evans against me, for one, and Coach Connover for another. Stu wants to keep the job and Steve wants him to."

"Mr. Connover won't want him to if you show you're as good as Evans. But, for the sake of argument, call it three to two, Tom. That's still a big margin."

"It might be if Steve didn't have a whole lot more to say than the whole bunch of us!"

"That's the point. It's up to us to see that Steve says what we want him to! That's where our wills get in their work. He may have more authority than you, or the three of us together, Tom, but your *will* is just as strong as his is!"

"Is it?" asked Tom startledly. "What do you know about that?"

"Of course it is. And you can make it stronger all the time by using it. In many of us the will power is merely dormant until we begin to exercise it."

"Well, it's all sort of mixed-up to me," said Tom. "Guess I'll never quite get the rights of it. But I'm willing to try the gag. What do I do first?"

"Quit joshing and talk sense," advised Clif impatiently. "Loring's got a good scheme, and it won't hurt us a bit to try it. Even if it doesn't get us anything it'll be sort of fun, sort of interesting."

"Joshing!" exclaimed Tom in hurt tones. "I wasn't joshing. I'm just as dead serious as the rest of you, but I've got to know what I'm to do before I do it, haven't I?"

"You've got to do what we've all got to do," answered Loring. "Tell yourself over and over that you're going to make an infield position on the second nine—"

"But I don't want just *any* position," interrupted Tom anxiously; "I want to play second base!"

"And keep on telling yourself that until you believe it. When you believe it others will. Work as hard as you can for that position. Keep in mind that Clif and I are thinking and believing and working with you every minute. Work and will, Tom. Let's go then! 'One for all and—'"

"All for fun," said the irrepressible Tom.

CHAPTER VII
A STRANGER LOOKS ON

THE FIRST TEAM DEFEATED Granleigh High School in a slow game marked by many errors on both sides and then played Murray School and lost, 7 to 2. Murray had a field day with the Wyndham pitchers, knocking Jeff Ogden out of the box in the third, by which time four markers had been put on the scoreboard, and hitting Sam Erlingby so hard that he, too, was wisely retired in the seventh. Although Murray made only three runs off Sam, he yielded six hits and three passes and was only saved from a worse fate by some really fast fielding at times. Sam was a right-hander and had been offered on the supposition that, since the enemy had severely punished Ogden, a left-hander, it would find a starboard artist more difficult. But Murray showed that he could hit them all, right or left, and gathered in thirteen hits in the process. Bud Moore, who pitched the game out, didn't escape unscathed, but he managed to keep the clouts scattered and witnessed no tallies. Wyndham looked feeble that afternoon as an offensive team, making but five hits off the opposing pitcher, two of which were credited to Captain Leland. Of Wyndham's brace of runs, one was put across in the second inning as a result of Wink Coles' single, an error by shortstop and Hurry Leland's two bagger into right. The other tally didn't materialize until the ninth, when the home team attempted a rally and, after Raiford had been thrown out at first, got Talbott and Van Dyke on second and first. Cobham, the Blue's catcher, bunted along the first base line and made the second out, advancing the runners, however. Pierce, batting for Bud Moore, drove a liner at second baseman, who fumbled long enough for Talbott to score. Van Dyke, though, was beaten by a few inches in his race for the plate, and the rally flivvered.

It was on the Monday following the Murray game that the second took the first into camp in a six-inning contest by a score of 6 to 5. The first's line-up was rather patched and was subjected to frequent alterations, but still it was the first team just the same and the second derived much satisfaction from that victory. Frost pitched for the scrub and did a good job, getting into many bad holes only to pull himself out by cool-headedness and canny judgment. Everyone on Mr. Wadleigh's roster got into action at one time or another, and Clif made his first hit against an opposing team in the eighth when he smashed a red-hot liner past Tyson, at third. Tom was again tried at the last corner and made two assists, but his only trip to the plate resulted in a fly-out to shortstop. Needless to say, he forgot all that Tusks had tried to teach him as soon as the first ball had been pitched to him and his batting form reverted to his famous imitation of Clouter Hearn.

Reminded of this by his fellow members of the Triumvirate that evening, Tom was at first impatient and then dejected. "It's no use," he declared finally in extenuation. "I mean well, but I just can't get the hang of it."

"But you don't remember," said Clif. "You start all right, and then you forget and back away and crouch. You don't keep your mind on the job, Tom."

"Well, why won't he let me hit the way I want to? Heck, if I ever coach a baseball team—"

"That's got nothing to do with it," interrupted Clif. "Tusks may be all wrong, but he's the boss and it's up to you to do what he tells you to do."

"But I forget!"

"You mustn't forget," Loring assured him earnestly. "When you forget it's because you're not doing as you agreed to do. You're not putting your mind to work. Now what were you thinking about when you were at bat this afternoon?"

"Thinking about?" Tom ran his fingers through his hair in puzzlement. "Why, part of the time I was wondering what Moore was going to shoot at me, and part of the time I was wondering if I could hit it, and part of—"

"There! That's just it! You had the wrong thoughts all the while. You should have been concentrating on the thought: I am going to hit it! You shouldn't have wondered about anything. Wonder means doubt, and you don't doubt, you *know!*"

"Oh, I do, do I? Is that so? Well, let me tell you I didn't know! And you wouldn't have known, either. That guy's got a mean hook, and if you don't know when it's coming you're a gone coon! Besides that, suppose I'd done all that concentrating you talk about; all that 'I-know-I'm-going-to-hit-it' stuff; how would that have helped me to stand up-close to the plate and put my feet together and all the rest of it? Huh?"

Tom was a dull student, and frequently very trying to Loring and Clif. Much valuable time was spent in pounding the philosophy of the "Work and Will" idea into his marble dome. Tonight, as on several preceding occasions, Tom agreed to mend his ways and promised to "trot out the old Will Power." So far no appreciable results had accrued to the Triumvirate from its campaign of "Work and Will," but, as Loring pointed out, a week was too short a time to prove anything. Besides, it was probable that none of them was yet concentrating and willing as effectively as he might with more practice. It doubtless took some time to warm up a fellow's will power and get it "hitting on all six."

Loring attended practice nearly every day. With the excellent Wattles as chauffeur, the chair was wheeled across to the second team diamond and installed in a sunny corner near the end of the stand and about opposite first base. It was a location from which Loring could watch the plate and the infield equally well, and its one disadvantage was due to the frequency with which foul balls invaded it. Loring himself was not at all troubled by that disadvantage, but Wattles was on tenterhooks constantly. Wattles was almost certain that he could catch a baseball if it came within reach, and there were moments when he would have welcomed a chance to prove his ability. But there were many more moments when he devoutly prayed that no such opportunity would be afforded him. Wattles was a dignified person, and the fear that he might, in spite of what was almost a conviction to the contrary, fail to make the catch and thus lose his dignity and become a laughing stock filled him with dread. Every time a ball glanced from a bat Wattles shot a hand to the brim of his black derby, stiffened with suspense and prepared to sell his life dearly.

During practice Loring had many visitors. He was well liked and thoroughly respected. There was, however, in spite of his friendly countenance, something about him that deterred merely casual acquaintances from claiming the privileges of friendship. Mr. Wadleigh always walked over and talked a moment, and so did several of the others from the bench. Frequently one or more friends would occupy the bench at his elbow and keep him company during part of the practice. Later, when he and Wattles followed the second team to the first team diamond, Coach Connover approached for a few words, or Hurry Leland or Pat Tyson paused a moment coming off the field. Today, the Thursday after the Murray game, a warm, sparkling mid-April afternoon, a stranger to Loring seated himself a few feet away on the first row of the stand. He was a fairly tall, bonily-thin man attired in a loose suit of gray tweed that had undoubtedly seen service and seemed somehow to have gained honor and distinction in the process. Loring's glance of uninterested inquiry became a somewhat prolonged study. The stranger's face, like his body, was thin, with high cheek bones and a rather more than adequate nose. The skin was sallow, pronouncedly so, yet did not suggest unhealthiness. Nor did the many tiny wrinkles about the eyes and around the corners of the mouth suggest age. The stranger was, Loring decided, no more than thirty-six, or, well, thirty-eight at the most. It was difficult to guess with certainty the age of those wiry, thin men. This particular specimen looked as if he had seen a good deal with those bright, brown, half-veiled eyes, and Loring could imagine him looking quite as much at home on the back of a swaying camel or huddled in an Arctic shelter as he did here, leaning forward, slowly revolving a cane between his knees with thin, brown hands and gravely surveying the efforts of Jack Cooper to get a hit. The stranger interested Loring from the first glance, and he found himself hoping that the other would presently offer an excuse for conversation. But that hope seemed due to frustration, for the minutes passed and the sallow man watched the scene in silence. More than once, after that first look, Loring stole glances at his neighbor, something which, since the neighbor was looking away from him, was possible without detection. After one such glance Loring turned back puzzled by the absurd thought that, despite utter dissimilarity, there was—was—well, there was something about the stranger that reminded Loring of Wattles!

Of course it was absurd, for when he stole a look at Wattles there was no single feature of the latter which in the slightest manner suggested any feature about the stranger on the stand; and Loring's fancy was dissipated. But three minutes later, the stranger proving more of an attraction for him than batting practice at the net, and, Loring having stolen another surreptitious glance out of the corners of his eyes, the fancy returned with full force. Yes, sir, while you couldn't put your finger on the point of resemblance—although resemblance was too strong a word for it—you just couldn't look at the stranger without recalling Wattles! It was mighty funny!

Presently the second was called across to the other field, and Wattles folded up the seat which he had occupied, hung it on the handlebar of the chair and followed sedately with his charge. The stranger arose, paused to fill a pipe with tobacco and made his way from the stand in the wake of the wheelchair. Once out of his hearing, Loring spoke eagerly to Wattles.

"Did you notice the man sitting near us, Wattles?"

"Yes, sir," replied Wattles.

"Do you know who he is?"

"No, Mr. Loring, I can't say that I do."

"You can't say? Well, geewhillikins, Wattles, you either know him or you don't know him! Which is it?"

Wattles cleared his throat deprecatively. "Beg pardon, sir. What I meant to convey was that I do not know the gentleman's identity but that it's barely possible I've seen him before, sir."

"You have? Where?"

"That's just it, Mr. Loring. I can't seem to recall the occasion."

"You've probably seen him around here then."

"Quite likely, sir," agreed Wattles obligingly.

"Well, but—but do you think you did see him here? Or was it somewheres else?"

"I fancy it might have been somewheres else, sir."

"Wattles, you certainly are the prize package!"

"Thank you, sir."

The subject of this discourse chose a seat high in the third base stand, and Loring's opportunities for further observation were few since Loring and Wattles were well beyond first base and across the diamond. In the course of the five innings that ensued—the game went only to five since the first had a batting fest in the fourth and delayed matters—Loring forgot the interesting stranger. Recalling him again during supper, he decided to ask information of Tom and Clif, but other matters sidetracked his curiosity.

On Friday the stranger again made his way along the length of the stand and again established himself close to where Loring's chair was placed on the grass. Again, save for a gravely smiling glance of recognition on the stranger's part, nothing passed between them. The man seemed to like to watch the practice, and yet Loring would have sworn that he was fairly ignorant of base-ball; little puzzled frowns, momentary expressions of blankness convinced him of that. Once Loring caught Wattles observing their neighbor intently, and later he asked: "Well, solved the mystery, Wattles?"

Wattles shook his head. "No, sir."

"Still think you've seen him before, though?"

Wattles hesitated. Then he answered evasively: "Well, Mr. Loring, it's hard to say. One encounters so many persons, sir. And sometimes a likeness deceives one, sir. Oh, very frequently."

"What I like especially in you, Wattles," said Loring dryly, "is your frankness of speech, your—your communicativeness, I might say. One has only to suggest a subject to you, and you fairly burst into artless prattle. Nothing—er—secretive about you, eh, Wattles?"

Wattles merely coughed.

On Saturday rain descended in torrents from eight in the morning until well after eleven, and the first team's trip to Minster to play the Minster High School team was abandoned. Although the rain ceased before noon the field was too wet for practice, and so first and second team players found themselves with an unexpected holiday confronting them. A few scrub nines did slip and paddle around on the diamonds that afternoon, but the regulars sought other forms of recreation. There was a Douglas Fairbanks picture at the movie theater, and, after Tom had excitedly broached the scheme, he and Clif and Loring—without Wattles in attendance—went. Tom pushed the wheelchair, and, fearing to be late, whizzed Loring along at a reckless clip, with Clif reminding him of the existence of such things as speed laws. Loring might well have experienced nervousness during that journey had it not been that the sidewalks for most of the way were practically deserted. In fact, the only person encountered between the entrance of East Hall and what Tom called "the heart of the metropolis" was Loring's sallow and fascinating stranger. They passed him near the Inn, strolling imperturbably along with pipe in mouth, swinging his crook-handled cane. That tweed suit looked baggier about the knees than ever, but it still challenged criticism. As he passed he darted a twinkle of recognition at Loring before his gaze moved on to Tom, but made no other sign. For an instant Loring thought he was going to speak or at least nod, and he was disappointed when he didn't. He turned eagerly to Clif for information, and Clif, who had recognized the passer-by, supplied what he could.

"That's Mr. Cooper," said Clif. "Jack Cooper's father. You know Jack."

Loring found the information disappointing, and his interest in the stranger waned. One simply couldn't associate romance with the second nine's catcher, round-faced, freckled and eminently commonplace. After a moment he asked: "Is he living here?"

"Must be," was the answer. "I saw him dining at the Inn more than a week ago."

"Oh," said Tom, "is that the man your father pointed out? I remember him. But, listen, why doesn't Jack look after him? I've seen him mooning around alone two or three times. He passed me on the drive the other day, and blamed if he didn't look like he was downright lonesome!"

Further pursuit of the subject was prevented by their arrival at the theater, but that evening, recalling it, Loring announced to Wattles: "Well, another mystery is solved, Wattles. That man we were wondering about turns out to be the father of one of the fellows, the heavy chap who plays catcher for the second team, Jack Cooper."

Wattles paused in the act of smoothing Loring's light coat preparatory to putting it away and turned an expressionless countenance to the speaker. "He might be, sir," he said after a space.

"Might be! Hang it, Wattles, I'm telling you he is."

"Very good, sir."

Monday turned out to be no sort of day on which to watch practice inactively, and Loring remained indoors save for a brief journey to the post office to mail some letters. By Tuesday noon, however, the chill east wind of the previous day had departed, and the wheelchair was rolled again to the second team field, being overtaken and passed on the way by a violently careening Ford from the seat of which Mr. Wadleigh waved a greeting. Practice was well along when Loring, from his accustomed place behind first base, saw Mr. Cooper enter the stand and, although row after row of empty benches intervened, make his way to a seat some two yards distant from the chair. Loring experienced a return of the former interest, despite the fact that the stranger was no longer a mystery, and quite brazenly smiled a greeting. Mr. Cooper smiled back and nodded. No, it was more than a nod, it was a very courteous bow. But the gentleman didn't speak, and Loring, regretting his overture, turned his gaze hastily away. Some minutes passed during which the rap of bat against ball and the cries of the players constituted the only sound. Then, at last, a pleasant voice came from beyond the railing.

CHAPTER VIII
VACATION VISITS

ACROSS THE DIAMOND, CLIF and Jack Cooper stood together in a group of five fellows waiting to bat, and Clif, turning his gaze away from a moment's contemplation of Loring and Mr. Cooper conversing together, remarked: "Your father seems to like to watch practice, Jack."

The catcher turned an unapprehending face. "What did you say?" he asked. Clif repeated the observation and indicated the reason for it by a nod toward the first base stand. Jack's gaze followed the direction of the nod, but still he seemed unable to grasp the significance of the remark. "My father?" he asked rather blankly.

"Yes." Clif was patient with him. "He's over there talking to Loring Deane. Can't you see him?"

"Oh!" Jack looked again. Then he turned a puzzled regard on Clif. "That's my father over there, is it?"

"Well, isn't it?" asked Clif in surprise.

"Don't recognize him, Clif." Jack was grinning broadly. "But then he's gone and lost about sixty pounds, if it is he, and it's made a terrible difference in him!"

"You mean Mr. Cooper isn't—isn't your father?"

"Sure, Mr. Cooper's my father, but I never saw that wampus before in my life! Go on and bat."

A few minutes later Jack sought Clif to ask: "Say, how'd you get it into your bean that that guy was my father?"

Clif had to think a moment before he replied. Then: "I thought someone told me he was, but maybe I just faked it myself. You see, his name's Cooper, and he's staying at the Inn, and I thought of course—"

"I'd like you to see my old man," laughed Jack. "Just for the fun of it. He weighs close to two hundred, Clif."

"That's mighty funny," muttered the other. He was thinking of his mistake, but Jack misunderstood.

"I don't see anything very funny in it," he answered. "He takes after me."

Meanwhile Mr. Cooper and Loring were getting quite well acquainted over there. Mr. Cooper's introductory remark had been a question revealing his colossal ignorance of the intricacies of the national pastime, and Loring had secretly thought it strange that Cooper had allowed his father to remain so unenlightened. But he was glad to supply the desired information, and explained not only the point then puzzling Mr. Cooper but several others which arose later. Mr. Cooper moved nearer and leaned his arms on the railing. In doing so he brought Wattles into direct range and included him in the friendly smile which accompanied his next remark. Watching, Loring was then and there convinced of one thing. If Wattles recognized Mr. Cooper as someone he had seen before, Mr. Cooper certainly had no recollection of Wattles. He had a rather deep voice which, however, encompassed several tones. The end of a remark might and frequently did end half a dozen notes higher than where it had begun, a feature that Loring found both odd and interesting. He spoke somewhat deliberately but without any drawl; in fact, although uttered slowly, his words were distinct and crisp. He was, Loring presently decided, undoubtedly an American, but an American who had traveled much and whose speech and manner of speaking had been borrowed from many lands.

The conversation ranged from baseball to the school, and about the latter Mr. Cooper was frankly curious. He had not, it appeared, seen any of the buildings save from the outside. "Why," exclaimed Loring, "haven't you even been up to Cooper's—I mean your son's room, sir?"

"My son's room?" repeated the other, almost startledly.

"Yes, sir," said Loring uncertainly. "I thought—someone said— Aren't you Jack Cooper's father, sir?"

The gentleman shook his head. "Really, no," he answered. "Who, if you don't mind, is Jack Cooper?"

Loring, in some confusion, pointed him out—Jack's face at the moment was pretty well hidden behind the catcher's mask—and the man who wasn't his father looked at him for several moments. Then: "Fine looking chap," he said, "but we're not related. Sorry."

"But you are Mr. Cooper, aren't you?"

"Yes, but apparently not the right one." He smiled deprecatingly while Loring said hastily: "I guess it was Clif Bingham who told me you were Cooper's father. That was Saturday. I—we passed you on the street, sir."

"I remember. Bingham is the boy who was at the helm that day?"

"The helm? Oh, no, sir, that was Tom Kemble. Clif was the other."

"I thought I recognized them both here a bit ago. Isn't that Kemble standing by the cage thing?"

"Yes, sir, and Clif Bingham's playing out in the field; the middle one of the three."

"Playing center field, I believe." The statement was made questioningly, and Mr. Cooper looked quite pleased when Loring's nod indicated that he had named the position correctly. "I'm rather a duffer about this game," he went on. "Haven't seen much of it, you know." His tone was apologetic, and Loring, smiling, answered: "I'll just bet, though, you know plenty of other games, Mr. Cooper."

"Not so many. Golf, of course, and polo. I've played that a goodish bit."

"Really?" exclaimed Loring. "I say, that must be corking! I'm going to get dad to take me to the games next summer. You know, when the English team comes across. Are you—do you play on one of our teams, sir?"

"Oh, no. Most of my playing has been over in India and around there. I'm really not much good at it."

"I'll bet you are, just the same," declared Loring, sweeping the lean figure with his gaze. "And I guess you play a corking game of golf, sir!"

Mr. Cooper appeared pleased and somewhat embarrassed. "Why, thanks," he replied. "But corking's hardly the word for the sort of game I play nowadays. I dare say you, now, could give me—" Then he stopped abruptly, with a sudden contraction of his brows, and: "By Jove, that was stupid of me!" he added remorsefully. "Look here, I'm beastly sorry, my boy!"

But Loring was chuckling. "Please don't apologize, sir! Why, I like being—I like folks to forget. It's almost as if I really could do things like—other fellows, sir. You see, Mr. Cooper, if I was able to I'd do everything of that sort. I mean play golf and baseball and football and—I think, though, I'd rather play football than anything else. Do you like football, sir? Did you use to play it?"

"No, I never played football, Deane. Your name is Deane, I think?"

"Yes, sir, but—I'm generally called Loring by my friends," said the boy a little shyly.

"Thank you," said the other gravely. "I see that you really have forgiven me. I was going to say that I do like to watch a good football game, but I've been knocking about a goodish bit and I don't recall when I saw the last one. I think it was in France, though; and that was nine—no, say eight years ago."

"During the War?" asked Loring.

"Yes, the Tommies played quite a bit, and so did the Yanks. Not the same game, though."

"You were in the War, weren't you, sir?"

Mr. Cooper nodded. "Yes," he said. Loring waited for more, but no more came; and something in the man's expression told him that another subject would be preferred. A silence followed in which Mr. Cooper watched the players, and Loring, appearing to do the same, really saw very little of what was going on. He was thinking about the stranger, reviewing the conversation and wondering if it would be permissible to invite the other to his room. Although Loring had yielded thoroughly to Mr. Cooper's attractions he was aware that one member of the trio had accepted that gentleman with reservations. Loring couldn't see Wattles without turning his head, and he hadn't turned his head once since Mr. Cooper had broken the ice, but he knew without seeing that Wattles was not wholly approving. Perhaps that knowledge would eventually have strengthened his determination to issue the invitation, but just at the moment it caused hesitation, and before the hesitation had ended the second team took its bats and traipsed away to the other diamond and Mr. Cooper arose, said: "Good afternoon," smiled and went away, too.

Loring rather unjustly blamed Wattles. "Look here," he charged, "you were beastly uncivil, Wattles, and I don't like it."

"But I never said a word, Mr. Loring," Wattles protested.

"And I never said you did. But I'll bet you looked as sour as a lime. Don't think I don't know that—that frozen face of yours by this time! Look here, what have you got against Mr. Cooper, anyway? You know perfectly well that stuff about having seen him before is absolute piffle!"

"No, sir," replied Wattles firmly. "Asking your pardon, Mr. Loring, I am perfectly certain that I have encountered the gentleman previously."

"Where, then? And what of it? It wasn't in prison, was it?"

"I have never been in prison, Mr. Loring," stated Wattles with hurt dignity.

"Oh, well, hang it, I didn't say you had. Don't be an ass, Wattles. If you don't remember where you met him, you can't have anything against him. And I could tell that he had never seen you in his life; at least, doesn't remember it if he has! I'm going to ask him to call the next time I meet him, and I won't have you looking the way you looked today."

"Very good, sir."

Presently, trundling across the grass, Loring said: "Sorry I spoke crossly, Wattles."

"Thank you, sir," replied Wattles. "I regret having given offense, Mr. Loring."

"You didn't, really," laughed the boy. "It was just my rotten temper."

Wednesday, however, Mr. Cooper was not at the field, and on Thursday it rained, and as a consequence Loring didn't meet Mr. Cooper again for almost a fortnight. There was no practice for the second nine on Friday, for Spring Recess commenced that day after the last recitation. Only those living a considerable distance from school were permitted to leave before Saturday morning, however, and the Triumvirate spent Friday evening discussing their plans for vacation. Tom was to be Clif's guest until the following Saturday. Then he and Clif were to go to Tom's home in New Jersey, stopping in New York on the way to take luncheon and go to a theater with Loring. Tom declared that he was mighty glad he hadn't made the first team, after all, since if he had done so he would have had to remain at school. The first played four games during recess, the first one at home and the others away. Clif said he thought taking the spring trip with the nine would be more fun than going home. Loring agreed with him, and so, perhaps, did Tom, although he refused to acknowledge it. Loring introduced Mr. Cooper again as a subject of discourse, but the others were rather fed up on that gentleman and side-stepped.

Loring went off soon after breakfast in a big, shining limousine, a car of the make that Tom called a "Rolled Rice," with a liveried chauffeur in front and Wattles, immaculate in a silk-faced black overcoat and his famous black derby, sitting beside the boy, an impressive picture of Respectability. Wattles unbent for an instant as the automobile rolled away and lifted his hat to the group on the steps of East Hall while Loring waved his farewell. Wattles' lapse from his standard of decorum was induced by Tom's parting hail of "Toodle-oo, Wattles, old top!"

Mr. Bingham arrived an hour later, and Clif and Tom piled their bags into the back of the old blue car and then crowded into the front with the driver. The blue car wasn't a "Rolled Rice," but it refused to take anyone's dust—not that there was any dust today, however—and slipped across country to Hartford, the luncheon stop, and then on to Providence quite as expeditiously and probably just as comfortably as the other could have done. Clif took the wheel after lunch and Mr. Bingham retired to the rear seat to smoke several long cigars.

The week simply whisked itself away, and on Saturday the two boys said good-by to Mr. Bingham and boarded the train for New York. There Loring and Wattles awaited them at the station, and they were borne away to a big house uptown and a cordial welcome from Loring's father and mother. Mr. Deane was a pink-cheeked, military-looking gentleman who, in spite of his great wealth, seemed to have very little to do and enjoyed doing it hugely. He and the visitors were already good friends and shared a number of small jokes between them. Mrs. Deane was, according to Tom's frequently expressed judgment, a "pippin'." Clif, for his part, had more than half fallen in love with her at first meeting, and still adored her shyly. That was a wonderful luncheon partly because it consisted of just the beautiful indigestible things that boys crave after a strict régime of school and partly because they were tremendously hungry. After luncheon there was a quick drive down the asphalt surface of the avenue, a breath-taking lurch into a side street and a hurried alighting before the theater. And they just made it! Loring, borne by Wattles, had scarcely been seated in his chair in the front of the box when the curtain rolled up and the darkened house became a glow of golden radiance. After that, save for brief interludes, Clif forgot that he was in New York and that the time was the humdrum twentieth century. He was in Old France where a gallant gentleman with a stupendous nose made Romance real at last and defeated his enemies—all save one!—with flashing blade or nimble wit. Clif was half-way to Morristown in the train before he finally emerged from the glamour cast upon him by the play.

Tom's guardian, Mr. Winslow, lived in a modest frame house fronted by a few square yards of greening turf and two leafless, contorted mulberry trees. After the Deane mansion, Tom's home was a come-down, a thought occurring to both boys but uttered only by Tom. "Rather a hovel," he said as they alighted from a taxi, "but I warned you of that, Clif." Tom had a big room, sparingly furnished, at the top of the house, and Clif was to share it with him. It was chill and damp up there, for spring had not yet ousted winter from the walls of the old structure.

Clif declared that the room was very jolly and that everything was perfectly corking, but secretly he was pleased that there were but two nights to spend there. Mr. Winslow, who appeared at supper time, proved to be a square-set gentleman of some fifty years, with an outward affability that didn't survive Tom's first night at home. The evening proved rather a dull one, and, since Clif was thoroughly tired, he suggested bed quite early. Tom seconded the motion, but his guardian expressed a desire to talk with him and Clif ascended the stairs alone. Afterward, although he tightly closed the chamber door, the voices of Mr. Winslow and Tom floated up to him for the better part of an hour, and it was evident to the listener that all was not peace and amity below stairs. Tom finally appeared, sullenly angry, bitter of speech. Clif learned that Mr. Winslow was not pleased with the reports received from Wyndham, especially those having to do with Tom's work in his English course, and had been particularly nasty about it. "Says if I don't do better," growled Tom, casting a shoe noisily to the floor, "he's going to take me out of school! All right, let him! If he does I'll beat it away from here mighty quick. *He* won't see me, that's a cinch! I'll go right from Freeburg to New York and get into the Navy!"

"The Navy won't take you without his assent, Tom. You're only sixteen."

"I'll be seventeen next month, won't I? Well, then! And whose money is it, anyhow? You'd think, the way he goes on, he was paying for my schooling and everything! I'll bet he gets his share, the old grafter!"

"Don't call names," said Clif quietly. "As Cocky used to tell us last fall, 'Fight, but keep your mouth closed!'"

Tom eventually calmed down and retired for the night in fair temper, but the incident didn't increase Clif's pleasure in the visit.

Mr. Winslow retained an elderly woman of good family and former affluence, who had lost husband and affluence—with Mr. Winslow's assistance, Tom stoutly declared—at the same time, to keep house for him. She was no addition to domestic cheerfulness, although she did make an excellent dried-apple pie, her meager conversation being confined to what Tom called "post mortems." Recollection of the years before poverty had come to her invariably induced sniffles. Clif was rather sorry for her, but he did wish she would use a handkerchief more often!

On Sunday morning Mr. Winslow, Mrs. Pelton—the housekeeper—Clif and Tom seated themselves in a small automobile of a rare vintage and rolled decorously to an ivy-covered church. Clif had Mrs. Pelton on his left and suffered a good deal when, he having found the hymn for her, she lifted her voice in song. He was heartily relieved when the sermon began. Sunday dinner was a somewhat solemn meal and certainly none too appetizing. Clif never had liked roast lamb much, anyway, and this particular roast had a "wooly" flavor which did nothing to increase his liking. The dinner accomplished one beneficent end, though; it sent Mr. Winslow to sleep in the parlor. With sighs of relief the boys let themselves out of the house and sallied forth in quest of adventure. They didn't find adventure, but they had a good walk and returned to supper in better spirits. Tom rebelled against church in the evening, and his guardian, although disapproving, forebore to press the point and went off alone. Eventually bedtime came.

Very early in the morning they started back to Freeburg. Clif wondered if he would ever again be so glad to return to school as he was today!

CHAPTER IX
"THE OLD WILL POWER"

THEY REACHED SCHOOL WELL before Loring. He didn't return until nearly four, revealing that even a "Rolled Rice" can have tire troubles. After greetings and a few questions had been exchanged, Loring asked: "Look here, fellows, have you heard about Evans and Cox?"

Clif shook his head, while Tom said: "Sounds like a good ticket. I'll vote for 'em. Who are they?"

Loring, though, was too much in earnest to appreciate persiflage. "Don't you read the papers?" he demanded. "The *Times* had it yesterday morning."

"Do you mean Stu Evans?" asked Clif.

"Yes! He and Cox; Harold Cox, isn't it? They got banged up over on Long Island Saturday afternoon. They were in Cox's car, and a truck shoved them out of the road, and they went down into a ditch. Evans broke a couple of ribs, the paper said, and Cox got cut up sort of badly and hurt an arm!"

"Gosh!" said Tom. "Cox is the fellow with the long neck and whitish hair, isn't he? Say, that's too bad."

"Have they come back?" asked Clif.

"Here? No, indeed. They were taken to a hospital and then to Cox's home. They won't be back for a couple of weeks at least, I fancy."

"Too bad," said Tom again, but he said it more slowly, and an expression of uneasiness came into his face.

"That surely ought to put you on second," said Clif.

Tom nodded, but he looked troubled. "Look here," he exclaimed, "I don't like it! I wasn't keen about that will power business when we started it, and after this I'm off it for life!"

"But, Great Scott—" began Clif.

"If it's going to get fellows into trouble I'm through with it," declared Tom emphatically.

"But you don't mean that you think *we* had anything to do with it!" gasped Loring.

"Sure, I do! Why not? Weren't we all putting our minds on getting on the team? You and Clif and me? Well, look what happens! Stu Evans gets laid up so he can't play! If that isn't up to us and—and our 'Work and Will' stuff, I'll eat my hat! And that guy Cox was an outfielder, wasn't he? Huh?"

"I don't know what he was," replied Clif, frowning. "He never played much, I guess. He was generally on the bench. Anyway, you can't say his accident helps me any! And, as for the other—"

"Sure, it helps you! You've got one less fellow to fight, haven't you? How do you know Tusks didn't have Cox in mind for one of the outfield jobs? No, sir, I'm through. There are some things—forces, or whatever you want to call them—that we don't understand, and it's a mighty safe thing to let them alone!"

"But, Tom, for the love of limes," exclaimed Loring, "think a minute! We didn't put our minds on Evans and Cox. We were willing Mr. Wadleigh to—"

"It doesn't matter," interrupted Tom stoutly. "The thing got away from us, I suppose. It didn't stop at Tusks. It went on and slammed those two fellows into a ditch. Why, heck, there's no telling what it might do next! First thing we knew there might be an influx, or whatever you call it, of measles or—or typhoid or something and the whole blamed batting-list would be nix!"

By degrees they argued him away from his conviction, but it required time and eloquence, and even after they had succeeded it was evident that Tom retained mental reservations and was only partly reconciled with the psychology program. A few days later it was learned that neither of the absent players had been seriously hurt, but the fact remained that they were both lost to the second team for several weeks. On Tuesday Tusks tried both Roe and Tom at second, and each showed so poorly, Roe at fielding and Tom at batting, that there was little to choose between them. When the second met the first Roe scored two errors, one a fumble of an easy liner and the other a wild throw over Scott's head. For his part, Tom accepted five chances well but was a miserable failure on his two trips to the plate.

The first team had met with two reverses during the recess, having been beaten by Hoskins and Goodwin. The two remaining contests had been won from Grayhold and Highland. So far, out of seven games, Wyndham had won four and lost three. Coach Connover, none too well satisfied, tried several new combinations in his infield during the week following vacation and, on Thursday, drafted Frost from the second to strengthen his pitching staff. The loss of Frosty left Mr. Wadleigh in something of a hole, for he had left only Purdy and a third-rate twirler named Ferry. Ferry usually played left field and confined his pitching to serving them up to the net in practice. Since the second had three games of her own scheduled for later on, Tusks began to look about for new talent, while the members of his team set up a loud howl of protest. None of them begrudged Frosty his good fortune, but they did wish he might have been left to the second. A boy named Fawkes, who had been pitching on one of the scrub nines, was given a try-out, but he showed small promise and was soon released. After that Ferry was taken in hand and groomed as an alternate for Billy Purdy. And Ferry, to the surprise of all and sundry, responded remarkably to the call to service. Relieved of the drudgery of pitching to the net every day, he remembered two or three tricky curves with which he had started out three years before to become a great twirler, brushed the cobwebs off them and, with Purdy standing by with advice, managed to make something of them. Ferry had no speed, but he had his curves and a fair degree of control, and on the first occasion of meeting with the big team puzzled the rival batsmen through three innings. The first got just four hits in those chapters. In the fourth, though, Van Dyke met one of Ferry's curves and slammed it for three bases, and after that Ferry went from bad to worse and gave way to Purdy in the fifth.

That afternoon Clif played a whole game through at center field. He made one difficult catch, misjudged another rather badly and, toward the end of the one-sided contest, heaved a fine throw from short center to Jack Cooper in time to catch a runner at the plate and retire the side. At bat Clif had no luck that day, knocking a short fly to third baseman his first time up, striking out the next time and hitting into a double the next. He would have come to bat again in the eighth, but there were two away and Connell was on second and Tusks sent Pringle in to pinch-hit. Clif somehow couldn't feel very sorry when Pringle hit at the first delivery and dropped a fly into the hands of Greene in center field.

By that time—the spring term was eight days old—Tom was established on second, for the present at least. Neither he nor the other members of the Triumvirate really expected him to retain his position after Evans' return, although they pretended to, for Stu not only fielded well but had a mighty good batting record besides. Tom's batting was still negligible; and that is speaking charitably. Once on base—and he did have a lucky faculty for getting to first by one means or another other than by hitting the ball safely—he was a fast runner and a heady one, and the number of runs credited to him after a fortnight's steady playing was quite out of proportion to his total of hits. On second base Tom played a snappy game, covering a good deal of ground and throwing well. He even enveloped himself in brief glory on two occasions, once by running well into right field for a Texas Leaguer that looked impossible and once by a sliding stop of a hard liner which he tossed over his head to Connell, covering the bag, and which Connell sped to first for a double play. He made errors frequently, but, as Loring pointed out, it was because he took so many chances.

Horner Academy was beaten, 4 to 2, in a well-played game, Ogden going the whole length in the box, and on the following Saturday Tollington High School was defeated in a contest requiring the services of Ogden, Frost and Erlingby. Frosty made his first appearance with the big team that afternoon and lasted only one and two-thirds innings, after going to the relief of Ogden in the fifth. Frosty seemed to have nothing on the ball, and he was hit to all corners of the field for two runs. Only some smart fielding and the fact that several of the batters hit flies to the outfield saved him from a worse fate. Sam Erlingby finished out and held the rampaging visitors to five more hits and two more runs. As Wyndham had started by stowing five runs away in her locker and had accumulated an average of one more for every succeeding inning, she escaped disaster, winning by 13 to 10.

If Tom's position on the second nine was precarious, Clif's was much more so. In fact, Clif could hardly be said to have a position. Ferry's withdrawal from left field to pitcher's box had resulted in the transference of Marler from center to left and the trying of various players in the middle garden. Burke, Deeker and Clif were experimented with. Deeker was eliminated in short order, leaving Burke and Clif to fight it out. There didn't seem much choice. Burke was as good a fielder as Clif; had played on the second last season and in consequence was ahead in experience; was equally as certain a hitter. Usually Coach Wadleigh started one and finished with the other. Infrequently one of the rivals played a practice game through. Clif, in spite of psychology, had a sneaking suspicion that Burke would eventually land the position. Of course when the old will power was working just right he could vision himself holding down the job unchallenged, but the old will power had a mean habit of developing engine trouble at times!

Shortly after the beginning of the new term Clif and Tom arrived at Loring's room one evening after supper to find another visitor ahead of them. The host, rather proudly as it seemed, introduced them to Mr. Cooper. Mr. Cooper appeared a trifle embarrassed as he shook hands, and for the succeeding ten or fifteen minutes had very little to say. Clif, recalling his father's indorsement of Mr. Cooper, was very friendly. Tom, however, perhaps because he had tired before this of Loring's frequent allusions to the gentleman, was less gracious. Without being in the least impolite, he nevertheless managed to suggest that he resented the presence of the outsider. Doubtless Mr. Cooper caught the suggestion, for more than once Clif found him observing Tom with studious intentness. Conversation limped for awhile. Even Tom was too courteous to introduce or pursue a subject which the stranger could not participate in or at least comprehend. Finally it was a chance word of Loring's that removed the restraint. Searching for a fresh line of conversation, Loring asked: "How did psychology work today, Clif?" Clif shook his head. That afternoon Burke had had rather the better of it. Then he turned to Mr. Cooper to ask: "I wonder if you believe in that stuff, sir?"

"Psychology?" said the man inquiringly.

Clif explained. "Yes, sir. Loring thinks you can get what you want by setting your mind on it and willing it to—to happen. You know, sort of out-thinking the other chap; making your will stronger than his and—that sort of thing."

"You ask if I believe in it? Why, yes, I do. After all, Mr. Bingham, there's nothing new in it, you know. History's full of it."

"Well," pursued Clif, "now here's a case, sir. Suppose you've got one person set on doing a certain thing a certain way and you've got three other fel—persons set on having him do it another way. Do you think that the three can make the first fellow do it their way by—by mental suggestion, or whatever you call it? I guess that's sort of mixed-up, the way I put it, but maybe you understand what I'm getting at."

"Yes, I understand, but I can't say yes or no to it. You see, it might depend on several things. First of all, I dare say, on whether what the three wanted was something very much opposed to the one man's—er—inclinations, something that in the natural order of events he wouldn't consider doing. For instance, there are three of you chaps. I might get out of this chair with the intention of walking to the door and going back to the Inn. If you three willed that instead of walking to the door I should crawl on my hands and knees you'd doubtless lose out for the simple reason that I am not accustomed to taking my departure in that fashion and would consider it—er—both uncomfortable and lacking in dignity. In that case a contest of wills would result in a victory for the minority."

"Yes, I see that," said Clif. "But suppose we just willed you to—let me see—to drop your hat and pick it up on the way to the door?"

"The odds would be shorter," replied Mr. Cooper, smiling. "I frequently do drop my hat, or my stick, or my gloves. In that case the result would probably depend on how strong your wills were. You might win if only because I, not knowing what was up, wouldn't actively oppose you. Care to try it?"

"Heck," said Tom, "you'd *know*, and of course we couldn't do it!"

"Yet I might," responded the other soberly. "I've seen several cases where mental suggestion, for want of a better name, has seemingly done strange things. I'll tell you of one, if you like."

"Yes, sir, please!" said Clif and Loring in chorus. Tom remained silent, but he looked as interested as the others. Perhaps Mr. Cooper had determined to overcome the slight antagonism still entertained by Tom, for all along he had seemed to address himself to Tom rather than to the others, and he continued to as he went on.

"This happened several years ago at a place called Canghall in the north of Scotland. A lot of us were stationed there after the War. We had a golf course of sorts near the garrison and played a good deal. Our best man was a chap named Brosser, a Major. He could wallop any of us, which wasn't so bad, but he got himself eternally hated by always reminding us of it. As a soldier he was a fine fellow, but as a sportsman he was a rank outsider. If you took him on he not only beat you hard but he kept bragging about it, before, during and after. I guess he was the most thoroughly detested player who ever sank a putt. It got so, finally, that no one would play with the swanker, and he had to offer all sorts of handicaps and odds to get a game. Things went on like that for a year or more. Then a few of us saw that something had to be done. One of the mess knew a young chap named Bedford who was then on leave of absence down in Kent. This Bedford, a subaltern, was a good golfer, but just how good we didn't know. Just the same, we decided to have a try with him. Well, we wrote to him and told him the lay and called on him in the name of all that was holy to come up for a week and slay the dragon.

"He came, and I liked his looks from the first. Rather a wispy lad, he was; long-limbed and awkward until you put a club in his hands. Very modest, too, and not at all sure he could turn the trick for us, but willing to try. It didn't take more than five minutes to arrange the match. The Major was tickled to death and went around telling what he would do to the youngster. Bedford played the course two or three times and then the match was on. The whole garrison turned out to see it. I don't suppose, unless it was his caddie, the Major had a 'rooter' in the crowd. But that didn't bother him a bit. I fancy he preferred things that way. Bedford didn't get his stride until they'd played four holes, and by that time the Major had him two down. Bedford wasn't in the Major's class with the driver, but he was a wizard with an iron, and not far behind the other on his putts. He got into his swing after a while and at the end of nine holes he was even up. From there on it was a ding-dong battle. They were both playing wonderfully good golf. If the Major won one hole Bedford won the next, and so it went to the fifteenth. Bedford won that. They halved the sixteenth. The seventeenth was long but not hard if you kept in the fairway. Your first shot laid you down in the narrows, as we called it. There was a point of forest coming in on your right and some ugly ground on the left, rocks and gorse. The Major had sailed through there a hundred times without trouble, and we all knew it. But we hoped. Afterwards, talking it over, we found that every last one of us had prayed that the Major would slice into the woods. You see, the rough on the other side wouldn't have done so well. With luck you could wangle out of there and be not much the worse for it. We'd all of us seen the Major get in there with a bad lie and still reach the green in par. So we all put our minds on the woods, and, since there wasn't a sound when the Major laid his brassie behind his ball, I fancy there was a deal of mental suggestion going on. Bedford had shot clean and sweet over the rise, and we knew he was all right. The Major looked a bit grim as he prepared to swing, but he didn't show any nerves. And then he hit."

"Well—well—" stammered Clif eagerly when the narrator stopped, "what happened, sir?"

"Why," answered Mr. Cooper, smiling, "what could happen? There was only one of the Major and a whole rabble of us. He sliced into the trees, lost ball, stroke, hole and match, two down and one to play!"

"Great!" approved Clif.

"And do you really think, sir," asked Loring, "that mental suggestion did it?"

"You'll have to decide that for yourself. That is, I think so, but the Major doesn't. He says he took his eye off the ball!"

CHAPTER X
"FIGHT! FIGHT!"

THE GONG WARNING THEM of study hour rang and Clif and Tom departed. Somewhat more than an hour later, however, they were back again. Naturally Mr. Cooper was the subject of conversation for awhile. Clif, too, had now fallen victim to the attractions of the gentleman, and he and Loring ventured numerous theories regarding him. "I'll bet," Clif declared, "he's seen a lot. He reminds you of one of those explorer chaps you read about and see pictures of, doesn't he? Look at the way he's all tanned up."

"I don't believe that's tan," said Tom. "I think his liver's on the fritz. Well, maybe some of it's tan, but—"

"I guess he must have lived in India," remarked Loring. "I met a man who lived there for a long time; represented an American oil company; and he had just the same sort of skin."

"How come he was in the English Army, though, if he's an American?" asked Clif.

"I don't believe he's an American at all," scoffed Tom.

"I do! Look at the way he talks. Not all the time, but usually. He doesn't talk a bit like Wattles."

"I think," said Loring gravely, "he's a Cosmopolite."

Tom was evidently in doubt as to what that was, but before he could ask enlightenment Clif exclaimed: "Well, whatever he is, he's a mighty nice sort. I like him. I suppose he's really quite old, but he doesn't seem so, does he? Do you suppose he's going to stay here right along, Loring?"

Tom made no objections to the recent guest as a topic of conversation, and even expressed an opinion himself now and then, but it was plain to be seen that he did not share the other boys' enthusiasm for Mr. Cooper.

The first nine began its mid-week games the following Wednesday, playing High Point School to an eleven-innings tie. Jeff Ogden was at his best that afternoon and went through eight frames without allowing a real hit. He was rather liberal with passes, but those, like Wyndham's errors, were scattered, and the opponent never got a man past second while he was on the mound. High Point's twirler was touched up for five hits in the same period, but none of the hits led to runs. There was some poor base running on Wyndham's part, and that, coupled with smart fielding by the invader, kept the home team scoreless to the tenth. Bud Moore, who succeeded Ogden, was hit more freely, and in the ninth two hits and an error by Captain Leland let in the first tally of the game and seemed to spell disaster for Wyndham. But the latter rallied in the last half of the inning and, through Raiford's double, Talbott's out to left fielder and a sacrifice fly by Van Dyke, evened up the score. Moore tightened in the tenth and held the enemy hitless, and after Wyndham had gone out in one, two, three order the game was called so that the visitors could catch a train.

With the first playing two games a week, the second nine met the big team only on Tuesdays, Thursdays and Fridays. There was never any game on Monday since Coach Connover devoted that day to furbishing up on the rudiments. On Wednesdays the second was generally released in time to witness the last four or five innings of the first's game, if played at home. On Saturdays, by the time May was half gone, the second held no practice at all. In consequence, when, three days after the High Point game, the first journeyed to Greenville, twenty miles distant, to meet Greenville Academy, most of the scrubs went along. Of the number were Clif and Tom.

Wyndham started Frosty in the box, and Greenville, by reputation a hard-hitting lot, took to his offerings with much enthusiasm. The visitor's outfielders nearly ran their legs off during that first inning and by the time the last man had flied out to Greene, in center field, four runs had crossed the plate. The Greenville rooters loudly demanded the removal of Frost and did a good deal of jeering, and Frosty was evidently far from happy during that opening. Nevertheless Steve sent him out again for the second inning, in spite of the fact that Wyndham had failed to even reach first base, and, after passing the first batsman, he settled down somewhat and pitched fairly good ball. With two out a long fly into left field escaped Talbott and the runner went all the way to third. He scored a minute or two later when Wink Coles juggled the ball long enough to let the batter reach first. After that Frosty worked the next man for two strikes on wide curves, pitched him two balls and then fooled him on a slow one.

The game went at 5 to 0 until the fourth. Wyndham was finding the Greenville left-hander a tough proposition, but in the fourth two singles together put Hurry Leland on second with one away and when Raiford was safe on first on a close decision the bags were all occupied. Talbott, however, failed to come through and made the second out, second baseman to first, and it was up to Van Dyke. Van found himself in the hole after three deliveries and then watched the fourth go past for a second ball. He spoiled the next by fouling it into the stand. Then he swung and hit cleanly into short right, scoring Hurry and Pat Tyson. When, however, he started to steal second a moment later the signals went wrong and a quick peg to third caught Raiford flat-footed.

Greenville added two more runs to her score in the fifth, although the one hit she made, a hard liner that Coles allowed to get through him, came with two down. The runner made second without trouble and went to third when Frost pitched his first delivery over Cobham's head. Frosty cracked badly then and passed the next batsman, who promptly stole to second. When he had tossed three balls and no strikes to the following player he was retired in favor of Erlingby. But Sam couldn't keep the bases from filling, and when Van Dyke failed to get a liner just inside of first two runs crossed. Sam struck out the Greenville pitcher, and a bad inning was over.

In the seventh Wyndham got two on after Cobham had fouled out and Erlingby had fanned, but they died when Captain Leland proved an easy out at first. Greenville added her eighth and last tally in her half of the inning, and Wyndham tried desperately to stage a rally in the first of the next chapter, and did get one lone run after Raiford had bunted, Talbott had sacrificed and Van Dyke had hit a short fly back of third. In the ninth, although Steve introduced a pinch hitter for Coles, who had had no luck at all against the Greenville left-hand artist, not a man reached first, and the Dark Blue went home tagged with her fourth defeat.

Clif and Tom had not found the game much to their liking and were rather disgruntled when they left the stand with some three score of their school-mates. So, when a loud-mouthed youth carrying a green megaphone and wearing a funny green-and-white skullcap forced himself on Tom's attention, Tom edged out of the throng and sought adventure. Although the Greenville partisan was a hunk of a boy and was well surrounded by friends, Tom displayed no hesitation. He walked up to the youth, seized the inadequate visor of his funny cap and pulled it down on his nose, stepped on his toe and said: "Is that *so*?" in a truly insulting manner. Clif and Jack Cooper reached their compatriot the next instant and strove to lead him back into the crowd, but Tom wouldn't budge. Greenville congregated rapidly. Innocent non-partisans were shoved and elbowed. In a moment Tom, Clif and Jack were hemmed in very solidly. Acrimonious debate began. The youth in the skullcap was outraged and said so loudly. Clif and Jack ingratiatingly apologized for Tom's hasty behavior, and Tom promptly declined to be apologized for. The enemy said something extremely uncomplimentary to Tom and accompanied it with a quick blow which, intended for Tom's head, landed on his neck.

After that events were very confusing. Clif found himself wedged against a painfully sharp plank, connected in some minor capacity with the grandstand, while a large, burly youth threatened him with a vague but awful fate if he didn't keep still. "You keep out of it," advised the big fellow. "Let your friend get what's coming to him." He grinned widely and appeared to bear no malice. Between the heads and over the shoulders of boys in front of him Clif could catch momentary glimpses of Tom and his adversary exchanging earnest blows. A few feet away Jack Cooper was trying hard to plow through the ring of observers, whether to take part in the fight or merely to secure an unimpeded view Clif couldn't tell. Farther away Clif saw the crowd become denser every moment. Cries of "Fight! Fight!" arose, and the efforts of those on the outside to get nearer were now seriously incommoding the battlers. "Keep back!" shouted the fortunate possessors of ring-side positions. "Don't crowd! Give 'em room!" Clif had a brief vision of Tom, smiling grimly, taking a wallop on one ear. Then, quite as if by magic, Tom disappeared and a roar of applause told the story. Clif struggled forward, now but half-heartedly restrained by the burly youth, and found himself able to see over a shoulder. Tom was getting up from the ground very slowly, very cautiously, his head guarded, and Clif sighed vastly with relief. The Greenville champion showed wear, but was evidently all for seeing it through. Tom was on his feet again, had rushed. There were sounds of blows. Clif couldn't see for a moment. Then he did see. The two were clinched, both raining ineffectual blows. A man, doubtless a self-constituted referee, forced them apart. Tom retreated. His opponent followed, feinting. Close to Clif's ear a voice bellowed: "Bore into him, Tom! Don't let him swing that right on you!"

The voice was Jack Cooper's. Maybe, above the many other voices, Tom heard it. At all events, he sprang forward, took a blow on his head and landed once, twice on the body. Green gave back and Blue followed. Tom ducked a wide swing and darted a straight right to the chin. It was short and they clinched again. Once more the referee parted them. Tom didn't retreat this time. He took punishment and gave it. Green left a wide opening and Blue shot a short jab to the face, ducked and planted a hard one on Green's ribs. Green faltered, looked worried, dropped his right for an instant and then it was all over. Tom swung up with his left, there was a sound like "*Ugh!*" and the referee jumped forward, an outstretched arm motioning Tom back. But Tom knew that his job was finished, and, while the audience still retained its attitude of neutrality, still shouted applause for the victor, he dived into the line where Clif and Jack were.

"Come on," he panted. "Let's beat it before they get sore!"

"I'll say so!" agreed Jack, put his shoulder against a neighbor and led the way. No one tried to detain them, although many stared and some applauded, and a moment later they were outside the crowd and the village street lay before them. Behind them the crowd was dissolving, still ahum with excitement. Small boys, surmising the identity of the hatless youth with the red, contused countenance, proclaimed their discovery loudly. Disapproving looks from scandalized but lingering citizens marked their hasty retreat. The bodyguard of urchins increased embarrassingly, and Jack threatened the leaders with dire things if they didn't "beat it." But that didn't prevail against the youthful hero-worshipers. They went ahead and behind and alongside, noisily discussing the event and the hero's personal appearance, the latter not always flatteringly. The trio walked as fast as they could, but the spectators of the recent fray had sighted them and set forth in pursuit. Clif looked back.

"There's a bunch of them," he announced uneasily. "They're running now. Gosh, we can't fight them all!"

"I guess they won't trouble us," said Jack. But his tone lacked conviction.

Tom drew a swollen hand from a pocket, turned and viewed the situation appraisingly. "If they don't make trouble they'll razz us like the dickens. How far's the station, Clif?"

"About four or five blocks, I think. Let's run, Tom."

"Aw, what for?" Jack protested. "I'm not afraid of that gang."

"You," replied Tom, "stay here and tell 'em about it. I'm off!" And so was Clif, and, after an instant, so, too, was Jack!

CHAPTER XI
TOM HITS A "JOLLY CRASH"

THEY TRIED TO GIVE the appearance of persons hurrying to the station to catch a train, but, since Tom was hatless and frequently applied a handkerchief to his flushed face, the imitation was far from perfect. When their course took them from the main thoroughfare Clif cast a look behind and announced that the pursuit had ceased, and they slowed to a walk, Tom puffing considerably. The station was in sight, a short two blocks distant, and as there was plenty of time they proceeded slowly, striving to regain composure before facing the eyes of their fellows.

"Say," asked Clif while Tom paused to examine his countenance in a window, "what the dickens did you do that for, anyway?"

"It was a patriotic duty," replied Tom. "Didn't you hear the nasty cracks that goof was making? Besides, I've always hated those idiotic caps that stick on the back of your head like a plaster!"

"Well, if you're going to light into every fellow who criticizes our team," Clif grumbled, "you'll have to travel alone. Gosh, you might have started a regular riot!"

"Well, I didn't. And anyway that hunk of cheese will keep his thoughts to himself for awhile, I guess."

On the train Tom sought a water cooler and performed first aid to his face. But he did not, of course, escape observation, and, while he was reticent and Clif vague, Jack, not having been bound to secrecy, gladly entertained an enthralled audience with a dramatic and highly colored narrative. Regret at having missed the event was loudly expressed on all sides. Pat Tyson, of the first team, was plunged into a dejection that lasted all the way home. Admiring friends clustered about Tom and gloated over the evidence displayed by his battered face, and a few were inclined to be rather peevish because he had not tipped them off to the fracas beforehand. It was generally conceded that it would be an excellent plan for him to remain out of sight of Mr. Connover, who, if a coach, was also a faculty member, and so Tom settled himself as far as possible from that gentleman, with his back turned, and played it safe. Yet luck was against him, for when the hour's journey was almost over Steve arose and strolled to the water cooler at the rear of the car. There, having appeased his thirst and exchanged a few words with Al Greene, across the aisle, his glance wandered to Tom. Tom was gazing absorbedly from the window, and continued to so gaze until, thinking that the coach had returned to his seat, he glanced about to make certain. Whereupon Mr. Connover spoke solicitously.

"What's the matter with your face, Kemble?" he asked.

Tom feigned surprise and passed an inquiring hand over it. "Must be dirt, sir."

"It doesn't look like dirt." Mr. Connover shook his head slowly. "Rather looks as if you'd had some sort of an accident." Clif, at Tom's side, gazed steadily at the brass knob on the car door.

"Oh!" said Tom, enlightenment in his voice. "That, you mean? Yes, sir, I—I did have an accident, sort of."

"Ran into something, perhaps?" asked the coach gravely.

"Yes, sir, I—ran into—something."

"Hm, something rather hard, too, I'd say. Perhaps you turned a corner too soon. If I were you, Kemble, I'd go to my room at once and fix that up. You'll find arnica helpful. And it might be a good idea to use some talcum before going to supper."

"He's a good scout," muttered Tom as the coach retired.

Although he followed the advice carefully, the result was not all he had hoped for, and whenever during supper he glanced up—which was infrequently, since he kept his head well down most of the time—he invariably encountered winks and grins. Also, he was made uncomfortable by the certainty that Old Brad, the Greek and Latin instructor, presiding at Table 13, was studying him with a suspicious eye. However, all's well that ends well, and nothing unpleasant came of his indiscretion. By the next morning, save for an area of discoloration which no amount of powder would hide, his face was normal. As for the similar spots on his ribs, those fortunately didn't show!

By the middle of the following week Mr. Cooper had become a frequent caller on Loring after supper time. It became quite the usual thing to find him there when Clif and Tom went over from dining hall, and Clif, for one, was disappointed when he wasn't there. Sometimes he played chess with Loring or Tom, but he was no master of the game, and generally the hour or more between supper and study hour was spent in talk. Mr. Cooper still remained something of a mystery, for none of the Triumvirate was rude enough to ask questions. They did learn quite a little about him, but their information came to them in unrelated fragments. They learned, for instance, that he had been in many countries in many capacities; in South America, at Bahia and Pernambuco; in India at Bombay and as far north as Kashmir; in Italy at towns they had never before heard the names of; in England and France and Germany and other countries as well. Once—that was before the World War—he had served in Algiers with the French Armée Coloniale. After the War, as he had told them earlier, he had been in the English Army in Scotland. What had gone between they didn't discover then, although they knew he had seen service. Lately, how lately was not established, he had been in British Columbia; he referred to it as "B.C." and confused Tom horribly. These facts appeared casually in the course of reminiscences. He never appeared to be trying to impress them with his experiences. Something reminded him of an incident, and he told it carelessly but always interestingly. His very manner of dismissing a whole glamorous land with a word or a phrase was in itself fascinating to the audience. But he was not always reciting yarns. More frequently he was listening to the doings of the boys, chuckling over the funny happenings of the day or giving grave attention to their problems. He showed no preference for any one of them, although he and Loring, seeing each other nearly every day at the field, had attained to an intimacy not wholly shared by Tom or Clif. Sometimes Clif received the impression that Mr. Cooper laid more store by Tom's interest or applause than on his or Loring's; but that was probably because Tom had shown himself more difficult. That Tom was gradually growing to share his companions' hearty liking for Mr. Cooper was soon apparent. And that respect went with liking was proved by something which happened one evening that week.

Tom had played a very good game at second base that afternoon, which, since the former incumbent of the position, Stu Evans, had returned to school two days before, was considered most fortunate. Stu wasn't yet in condition to play baseball, but he soon would be according to report, and the Triumvirate were hoping—and willing—that Tom would meanwhile prove his right to retain the position. But they realized that he wouldn't do so unless he improved his hitting considerably. That was dwelt on this evening, and Tom grew quite pathetic over his inability to get a hit off the first team pitchers. "That's what's going to queer me," he said sadly. "That fellow Evans doesn't have to play second any better than I do, because he's got the edge on me when it comes to batting."

"What I can't understand," said Clif rather hopelessly, "is why you don't get onto yourself. Tusks shows you how to bat his way and you say 'Yes, sir,' and then go right on giving your famous impersonation of Clouter Hogan, or whatever his silly name is!"

"My sainted Aunt Jerusha!" exclaimed Tom despairingly. "Haven't I been telling you that I'm mighty near worn out trying to remember to do like Tusks says? I just can't, that's all! I get so balled up trying to think what it is he wants that I can't hit the ball, and then I forget his way and swing like I'm used to swinging, and still I don't hit it! Heck, I'd—I'd do it if I could!"

Mr. Cooper said, in his quiet way: "Kemble, if I were you I'd stop thinking about it entirely, and when it came my turn to bat tomorrow I'd just step up and do it."

"Huh?" ejaculated Tom.

Mr. Cooper smiled. "The quickest way to do a thing is to—*do* it. Try it tomorrow."

Tom opened his mouth, closed it again, cast an inquiring glance at Loring and relapsed into thoughtful, somewhat puzzled, silence. Loring swung the conversation to another channel, and baseball was not mentioned again that evening. During the quarter of an hour or so that passed before the gong rang Tom was noticeably detached.

The next afternoon, at the field, Wattles said: "Mr. Kemble certainly hit it on the nose that time, didn't he, sir?" Wattles was acquiring quite a baseball vocabulary. Loring started and looked around.

"What did you say about Tom?" he asked.

Wattles repeated his observation with relish, adding: "I fancy you didn't see it, sir. He took quite the approved stance and gave the ball a jolly crash, Mr. Loring."

"Probably you mean smash, Wattles. No, I didn't see it, but I'm glad to hear it. Do you mean that he stood up to the plate, like the others, and didn't crouch?"

"Absolutely, sir. I was quite surprised!"

Loring chuckled. "So I'd have been if I'd seen it. I was wondering what's happened to Mr. Cooper today. He has seemed so interested in Tom's try for second that I was sure he'd be out this afternoon. Perhaps he thought it was going to rain. It did look like it awhile back, but———"

Loring's ruminative flow was abruptly checked. Slim Scott had knocked a foul into the air, and the descending ball was making straight for the wheel-chair. There was a desperate ejaculation from Wattles, his stool fell backward and there was a loud *smack* as the sphere struck his cupped hands and—mar-vel of marvels—stayed there!

"Fine work!" exclaimed Loring gleefully. An audience of two score on field and stand laughingly applauded, and Wattles, his long countenance express-ing mingled surprise and triumph, stepped forward and with a sweep of his arm bowled the ball toward the pitcher. There was a sharp exclamation of dismay from that youth as he sprang nimbly aside, and the bounding missile sped on into the outfield.

"Well bowled, sir!" shouted Tom from the bench, joyously. "Oh, very well bowled, sir!"

Wattles resumed his seat with dignity, resettled his disturbed derby, wiped his hands with a handkerchief and tried very hard to look as if nothing had happened. But he didn't succeed, for the feat had left a glow of exaltation on his countenance. He had faced the oft threatened crisis, had met it, had won! There was, in fact, a new and strange light in his eyes as he rubbed his tingling palms gently together, such a light as may perhaps have shone in the eyes of Columbus as he first sighted the shore of a new continent!

"Gee," said Loring enviously, "I wish I could have caught that, Wattles! Say, I'll bet it felt good, didn't it?"

Wattles cleared his throat. "Er—yes, sir, I think I may say that the sensation was surprisingly agreeable."

After that whenever a ball was pitched to a batsman in front of the net Wattles became tense and expectant. But although fouls were frequent they usually struck the hood of the net and not again was Wattles allowed to experience the agreeable sensation.

When Tom made his second trip to the net Loring was sorrier than ever that Mr. Cooper wasn't on hand, for Tom behaved most remarkably. Instead of standing away, with widespread feet, and crouching, he stood straight, almost toeing the rubber. And instead of waving his bat around continuously he kept it almost still. Doubtless Clouter Hearn would have wept or gnashed his teeth had he been there to see! Having disdainfully allowed the first offering to pass him, Tom met the next one and hit it straight over second. A moment later he lifted a fly to short left, and then, to complete a perfect exhibition, bunted nicely.

Scarcely crediting his eyes, Loring shouted his delight so loudly that even Tom, making his way back from the plate, heard and waved. "What do you think of that?" Loring demanded of Wattles. "He hasn't hit like that all season! Wasn't that corking, Wattles?"

"Oh, quite, sir," replied Wattles warmly. "He certainly poked out a remarkably nice bingle, Mr. Loring."

There was great rejoicing amongst the Triumvirate that evening, and Clif spoke for all when he said: "Gee, I wish Mr. Cooper was here with us!" But Mr. Cooper didn't appear and so didn't hear Tom's frank acknowledgment of indebtedness to him.

"You see," he explained earnestly, "I got to thinking over what he said last night; about the right way to do a thing being to *do* it, you know. Say, there's a whole lot in that, fellows. He said a mouthful! Well, I got to thinking about it, as I said before, and I just made up my mind that I'd quit all the funny business, all the psychology stuff and the 'I-Will' rot, and—"

"Do you mean," demanded Loring in pained tones, "that you didn't—didn't have your mind on—"

"You bet I didn't," answered Tom triumphantly. "I didn't use my mind at all. I didn't think about anything! I just stepped out there and walloped the old apple!"

"But you must have subconsciously determined—"

"I didn't even think of the old subconscious," declared Tom brutally. "I tell you I kept clear of all that stuff. I—"

"Hold on a minute," laughed Clif. "Just awhile ago you said you 'made up your mind to quit all the funny business.'"

"Huh?" said Tom blankly. "Well, but, hang it, that was last night! Today I didn't make up my mind to anything! I didn't have any mind! That's why I came across, I'm telling you."

But Loring was smiling again. "It's perfectly simple," he explained. "You made up your mind last night what you were going to do today. So, of course, you didn't have to think any more about it this afternoon. See what I mean? You've got your will power working so perfectly now that it's good for twenty-four hours, Tom!"

"I have?" Tom looked startled at first, and then very proud. "Is that how it was? Just like a clock, eh? I wind it up tonight and it runs until tomorrow night? Say, that's great! I always suspected I had a grand little mind!"

"Never mind your grand little mind," said Clif. "What we want to know is whether you can keep it up. Hitting the ball, I mean, and hitting it the right way."

"Sure, I can! Heck, there's no trick to it after you learn how."

"Still, I noticed you got only one hit off Sam Erlingby in three times up."

"What of it? That hit was a humdinger, wasn't it? Tyson didn't get within three feet of it! The other times Sam fooled me with a slow one once when I was up, and then Tusks told me to bunt and Sam kept them all low the next time. Heck, that's no—no criticism!"

"You mean criterion, I suppose," said Clif, "but never mind. Just you keep it up, Tom, and Stu Evans will have to whistle for his job. I don't care an awful lot for that chap, anyway. It was sort of hard luck, his getting banged up like that, but he shouldn't have been joy-riding with Cox. Anyone could see that Cox couldn't drive a car! You keep right on winding up the old will power every night, Tom, and you'll be a ball player yet!"

"Is that so?" asked Tom with stinging sarcasm.

CHAPTER XII
THE BATTLING FLIVVER

TOM ROOMED WITH BILLY Desmond, a second class fellow. Billy was both a football and crew man, this spring rowing at four on the School eight. The baseball team played away from home on Saturday, meeting Peebles School at Clear Lake, and after what had happened last week neither Tom nor Clif was enthusiastic about going along. Still, they probably would have gone if the crews hadn't offered an attraction nearer home. First and second eights were to do battle over the short course against similar crews from Highland School, and, since Billy was to row in the first boat, Tom proposed attending the races rather than the baseball game. Clif was agreeable, but mentioned the fact dubiously that Double Lake was nearly four miles away from the entrance of West Hall.

"Heck, I'm not suggesting that we tramp it!" said Tom. "Far, far from such, old scout. There's a fellow in the village who's got a beautiful flivver, and I'm pretty sure I can get him to take us over and back for a couple of dollars."

"You mean that chap who drives the 'The Wreck of the Hesperus'?" exclaimed Clif, outraged.

"Sure. Why not? The thing goes all right, so what do you care how it looks?"

"We-ell, but you're sure we can't hook a ride with one of the crews. Those busses hold—"

"I know how many they hold, but there isn't a chance. I asked Billy if he couldn't smuggle us aboard, and he said nothing doing. Say, if it's the dollar that's worrying you, cheer up. I'm flush, boy!"

"No, I'm not worrying about the dollar, I'm worrying about my self-respect," answered Clif. "All right, though. I'll sacrifice even that for you, Tom. Hold on, though! Say, I wonder if Loring would go."

"Loring? Gosh, I don't believe so. Still, he might. That would mean taking Wattles, too, though."

"Leave Wattles at home. As long as the car held together Loring would be all right. Let's ask him."

They did, and on Saturday afternoon "The Wreck of the Hesperus" rolled away from West Hall amidst the loud cheers of a hastily assembled audience.

Wattles watched the departure with very evident disapproval and anxiety. In his opinion "The Wreck" was not a seemly conveyance for the son and heir of Mr. Sanford Deane to be observed in. And, besides, the contraption appeared to be on the verge of dissolution. No anxiety troubled the occupants of the ancient and dilapidated Ford, however, as it fled down the driveway and lurched, with a convulsive shudder, into Oak Street. The driver and owner, one Augustus Meggs, otherwise Gussie, was employed at a local garage as a mechanic. Gussie was about twenty, was long and angular, had a freckled face and remarkably prominent ears and chewed gum as a life work. He was always willing to tell how he had bought the car for eighty-two dollars three years before and had "remodeled her, by crickey" with such odds and ends as were to be found from time to time around the garage. Tom referred to Gussie as the "Skipper" and conversed in nautical terms with him all the way to the Lake. Gussie didn't understand him much of the time, and was fully aware that his employer was having fun with him, but he didn't mind. He had held out for three dollars and got it, and for three dollars anyone could make fun of Gussie as much as he pleased. Secretly Gussie was of the opinion that the joke, if there was one, was on the passengers!

They made Double Lake without misadventure, the skipper of "The Wreck" taking things sort of easy after it had been explained to him that the boy who had been carried to the car was so brittle that he would fall to pieces if bounced around too hard. In fact, the skipper drove so cautiously that by the time the old Ford wheezed down to the boathouse landing the junior crews were already up at the start. It was a warm but blowy afternoon, and the blue waters of the lake were tipped with whitecaps. About fifty Wyndham youths, congregated around the boathouse, were cheering themselves red in the face, and after finding Billy Desmond and assuring him of their support, Clif and Tom returned to "The Wreck of the Hesperus" and bade the skipper warp his craft closer to the cheering section. Its arrival there met with loud acclaim, even the crews being for the moment forgotten by the cheerers. Gussie received the applause modestly, found a fresh piece of gum in a pocket of his flannel shirt and substituted it for the wad which had done such good service on the trip out, placed a stone under one of the back wheels—the brakes didn't work very well, he explained—and joined the crowd. And just then the report of a pistol half a mile distant came faintly, and the cheering section broke into a confused medley of incoherent entreaties: "Come on, Wyndham!... Row, you dumbbells!... Hooray! Hooray!... Hit it up! Hit it up!... Wyndham! Wyndham!... Come on! Come o-o-o-on!"

Wyndham was not looking for victory today. Until last year she had always put four-oared crews on the water and had won her share of triumphs. Last year, however, a generous graduate had given the school two new eight-oared shells, thereby somewhat complicating Wyndham rowing affairs. Horner Academy, the Dark Blue's chief rival on the water, was still sticking to fours, and it was therefore necessary either to give up Horner that spring or to let the new shells lie on the racks. Horner practically promised to have at least one eight-oared crew ready for the following season, and so, partly for that reason and partly because it would have looked like base ingratitude not to use the gifts, Wyndham changed from fours to eights, muddled through the early season without a race and finally entered her first crew in a three-cornered event on the Housatonic River and finished third only because there was no fourth entry. One of the Wyndham rooters declared bitterly that, after the winning crew crossed the line, he ate three hot dogs before the dark blue oars came into sight! Still later that spring Highland, which had been boating eights for several years, came down to Double Lake and inflicted a second defeat. But Wyndham rowed a better race that day and made the opponent hustle to show a length and a half of water at the finish. The Dark Blue had learned much since then, but graduation had taken her best oarsmen, and today, in the first boat, only Captain Badger, at stroke, and Billy Desmond remained of those who had trailed Highland. As for the second crew, well, it was hoped that a few of them would still be pulling when the shell reached the finish—always supposing, that is, it ever did reach it!

But the eight occupants of the second boat—nine if we include young Carter, the cox—thought better of themselves than that. They seemed to have an idea that if they kept on digging their blue-tipped sweeps into the water long enough they could win the race. Of course, since only half of them had ever rowed in a shell before, this was a most astounding idea; so astounding that even Mr. McKnight, chemistry instructor and assistant rowing coach, who had charge of them, stared unbelievably from the launch when the two slim craft ahead passed the half-way flag apparently even. "Lovey" passed a hand over his eyes and looked again. There was no doubt about it, though; the stern of the Wyndham boat was not a yard behind the stern of the Highland shell. Not only that, but Wyndham was rowing as steadily as her rival, putting a lot of power into a twenty-eight stroke! About that time Lovey McKnight forgot his dignity, both the dignity befitting a faculty member and the dignity becoming to a coach, and was heard by other occupants of the Wyndham launch to babble wildly.

Over on the shore, the group by the landing had broken up. Its members were sprinting along the edge of the lake, waving whatever they could find to wave, shouting at the top of their lungs. Not all of them, though, for a handfull elected to see the finish from the landing, and among these were Tom and Clif and, of necessity, Loring. They had a clear view, but the angle kept them in uncertainty of the boats' relative positions. Once it seemed that Wyndham had put a half-length between her and her rival, but a moment later they concluded that the boats were still practically side by side. The distance was a mile and a half, and at the mile flag both crews began to show the strain. Wyndham was splashing a good deal, and Number 6 in the Highland boat was rowing late and short. The Dark Blue hit up the stroke to thirty, to thirty-four, and seemed to gain for a time, but the Blue-and-White answered the challenge and eventually evened matters again. After that, to the watchers by the landing, it was anybody's race right to the finish. They saw Wyndham pulling fast and hard and raggedly, Highland desperately rowing a stroke of thirty-six or better. Saw the boats shoot in front of the farther flag, saw the oars trail and tired forms in each shell slump in their places, saw the following launches slow and turn; and still they were in doubt. It was not until the Wyndham launch had started back that Clif uttered a yell of triumph.

"We won!" he shouted. "We won! Look at those fellows!"

"Those fellows," by which Clif meant the launch's occupants, were, indeed, acting very much as though pleased at the result. One or two, Mr. McKnight and Weldon, manager and first class member, perhaps, were behaving decorously enough, but there were at least six others there and these latter were performing antics that threatened to take them overboard!

"My Sainted Aunt Jerusha!" howled Tom. "We sure did! We beat 'em, Loring! What do you know about that? Are we the eel's whiskers or aren't we? I'll say we are! I'll tell the world—"

"Shut up!" someone begged. "They're trying to tell us!"

A blue megaphone was pointing their way from the bow of the approaching launch. "Wyndham won," came the hoarse bellow. "By about a third of a length! A-a-ay!"

"A-a-ay yourself!" yelled Tom. "Wait till you see what happens to 'em in the next race!"

But something happened before the next race, happened almost while Tom was still shouting through his funneled hands. He and Clif and the dozen or so others who had remained about the boathouse had clustered either on the float or along the edge of the water to get the message from the launch. Loring, in the back seat of the automobile, had been left alone in his glory a matter of ten yards up the little grassed slope. Perhaps in his delight over the victory he stirred himself enough to jar the car, for there was a *snap* as the emergency brake released and a jolt as a rear wheel went over the inadequate stone placed before it. It was then that Loring's shout of alarm reached the others. Perhaps it would be nearer the truth to say that it reached Tom, for many voices were raised and through the babel Loring's voice carried no message to most of the group. But Tom heard, looked and realized. The crazy vehicle was rolling slowly down the slope, heading for the edge of the lake. With an able-bodied boy in it, Tom would probably have remained where he was and laughed himself to death, for the automobile, after pitching a bit over a few loose rocks near the margin, would doubtless drop comfortably over the two-foot wall and come to a stop with the water no higher than its floor-boards, and even if its occupant had elected to stand by the ship no harm could come to him.

But it was a different story with Loring in the car, and Tom didn't stop to laugh. He made a flying leap from the float to the low wall, hurling an inoffending youth head-over-heels in his flight, and charged up the slope. "The Wreck of the Hesperus" had started what she may have intended for her final voyage slowly and demurely, but with every foot traversed she had gathered speed, and when Tom reached her she was coming at a determined pace. He went up the slope with a yell that brought every head around, and on the instant other feet pounded behind his. But he couldn't wait for help, and he knew it. Nor did he dare to try to reach the brakes. All that he could do was charge into the little car, head down and shoulders hunched, just as he might have charged into an opposing lineman. There were no falderals on "The Wreck," no bumper to keep Tom from coming to close grips. He crouched and met the radiator with his left shoulder, digging his shoes into the sod.

But even as light a car as "The Wreck," when it has an occupant and has made a fair start downgrade, is not to be stopped in any such manner. Car and shoulder came together with a force that made every bolt and rivet rattle and that hurled Tom a foot away and almost lost him his footing. But he staggered back to the fray, charged again, putting every ounce of strength and weight into the effort, and won a momentary victory. The car didn't stop, but it did pause for an instant before pushing this strange obstacle before it again, and in that instant it lost some of its headway. And before it could gather speed again Tom had plenty of help.

One oversanguine youth seized "The Wreck" by a mudguard and promptly measured his length, the mudguard clattering about him. But others were more practical. Several joined Tom at the front while another leaped to the running board, slid into the car and applied brakes. "The Wreck" protested, bucked and abandoned her contemplated suicide. Gussie, his freckled countenance pale with emotion, swallowed his gum and came very near to strangling during the succeeding confusion. Clif had been too far distant to reach the car in time to be of use, but it was Clif who planted the first stone—no mere inconsiderable pebble this time—under a wheel and then jumped to the running board and anxiously faced a white but smiling Loring.

"Are you all right?" demanded Clif anxiously.

Loring nodded. He could smile, but he wasn't ready for conversation yet. He pulled the discarded rug back over his knees first, and by that time Gussie had recovered from his choking and the crowd was clustering thick about the back seat, laughing, though rather nervously, and plying Loring with questions. Tom was conscious of two things just then. One was that his shoulder hurt horribly and the other was that he wanted above all things to beat Gussie to a pulp. He showed a fine determination to perform this feat, using one arm only, when peace-makers interfered and the alarmed Gussie was rescued. One of the fellows who claimed a knowledge of Fords started the car, and, with the others ready to leap upon it and throttle it if it showed a continued tendency to go into the lake, maneuvered it up the declivity and onto level ground. Gussie had forgivingly offered his services, but Tom had refused to trust him. By this time the launch had joined the waiting Wyndham first crew and together they were going down to the starting boats, and the episode of the runaway Ford was forgotten by the throng, now enlarged by the return of many who had followed the first race alongshore.

"Guess we'd better go home," said Tom, scowling blackly at Gussie. "You must be all in, Loring."

"I'm not, really, Tom. And I want to see the other race. But perhaps we'd better go so you can have your arm attended to. It must be awfully bruised up."

"Heck, it doesn't bother me. What do you say, Clif?"

In the end they decided to wait for the final event, but a quarter of an hour later they regretted not having gone when Tom proposed going, for the Dark Blue's first crew, after getting the better of the start, was headed in the first quarter-mile by a smooth and powerful adversary and rowed off her feet—if the phrase is allowable here—before the mile was reached. After that, although Wyndham hung on doggedly, Highland opened water with every stroke and finished almost ten lengths ahead. "The Wreck of the Hesperus" returned to Freeburg at a slow and mournful pace, the apologetic but unforgiven Gussie very low of spirit. He had swallowed his last piece of gum.

CHAPTER XIII
TOM PAYS A CALL

BY GENERAL CONSENT WATTLES was not informed of the incident of the suicidal Ford. It would, as Loring pointed out, only upset him to learn of it. Loring tried very hard to thank Tom for his part in the affair, but Tom refused to be thanked and ridiculed Loring's efforts. "What's it all about?" demanded Tom. "What are you trying to do, josh me? Make him be good, Clif, won't you? I'm sensitive and get hurt feelings awfully easy!"

Tom's hurt feelings were really in the shoulder which had borne the brunt of "The Wreck's" charge down the hill, and his left arm wasn't of any use to him at all the next day, and of very little use on Monday, by which time it looked, according to Billy Desmond's description, like "one of those Italian sunsets painted by that—what's his name, now?—Turner!" During practice on Monday Tom lacked so much snap that, to his alarm, Roe was sent to second in his stead when the scrub played the first. Stuart Evans was out that afternoon, although not in togs, and seemed rather pleased when Tom was relegated to the bench. Across the diamond Loring and Wattles were occupying their usual position beyond the first base stand. Loring had bought a score-book and was learning the science of scoring. Cotter, one of the first team managers, had brought him the batting orders and was now leaning over the wheelchair, explaining something. Tom, watching rather moodily, noted that Mr. Cooper was not to be seen and recalled the fact that that gentleman had not been around for three days. Maybe he had taken his departure from Freeburg. Well, Tom couldn't blame him for that, but, just the same, he'd be sort of sorry if he had. Of course he wasn't nutty about Mr. Cooper, like Loring, but he did sort of like the old goof. Funny he wouldn't have come around and said good-by first, though. Well, folks were like that. Friendly enough when it pleased 'em, but—

Tom's morose meditation was interrupted by Pringle, a not very promising understudy for Slim Scott. Pringle moved up from further along the bench and squeezed down beside Tom. "Say, did you hear about Wattles, Tom?" he asked, grinning.

"Wattles?"

"Yes, Loring Deane's man there." Pringle nodded toward the other side of the diamond. "Say, it was funny!"

"It must have been," said Tom dryly. "Or maybe it's just the humorous way you tell it."

"No, listen. Saturday Linton and Cox and I took a walk and went over beyond town where the High School fellows play. Well, there was a game going on and we stopped to watch it. It was just sort of a scrub affair, you know. Some of the fellows who work in the stores. There was the guy who clerks at the Inn and the red-headed chap from the drug store—Burger's, you know—and a dozen others. I guess High School was playing away somewhere. Anyhow, these guys were having a great time, most of them playing in their shirt-sleeves. I wish you could have seen the fellow who was pitching! Honest, he was a scream. Well, presently Lin says 'Who's the tall whatsthis playing out in left? Don't he look like that Wattles fellow?' Well, sir, it *was* Wattles! He—"

"You're crazy," said Tom. "*Wattles!*"

"Cross my heart, Tom! Why, we stayed there and watched, I tell you. He had his coat and vest off, and, of course, that trick derby of his, and just at first I wasn't sure about him. He looks different without the old bean-pot. But it was him—I mean he, all right. He had on a pair of violet suspenders—"

"Not Wattles," corrected Tom gravely. "Wattles wears braces."

"Huh? Well, braces then. Ever see him with his vest off? Honest, Tom, his trousers come almost to his shoulders in the back. Funniest looking sight you ever saw! Well, we watched him awhile and it was good as a circus. Every little while some guy would knock a ball his way and Wattles would hold up his hands. Then he'd find out that the ball wasn't coming where he was, and he'd start to run, still holding his hands out, mind you! Funny? Boy, it was a scream!"

"Did he catch anything?" asked Tom, chuckling.

"Well, yes, he did get one fly, and it wasn't so rotten, either. But generally he just ran around out there, always yards away from the old pill when it lighted. He was so red in the face he looked like he was going to bust. And he was so blamed solemn all the time! Like he was performing—a—awhatyoucallit—rite!"

"It's a good story," said Tom approvingly, "but of course you're lying, Pringle. Old Wattles would no more slip out of his coat and chase around in his shirt-sleeves than—than—well, he just wouldn't do it, Pringle. Mind, I don't say the fellow didn't look like Wattles. He probably did, although, at that, Wattles has a peculiar and quite uncommon style of beauty—"

"Chase yourself," advised Pringle disgustedly. "It *was* Wattles. If you don't believe me ask the others. There's Cox right over there. Think I don't know what I see when I see it? Listen, Tom, honest it was Wattles!"

"Naughty boy," admonished Tom, smiling. "Mustn't tell fibs. Papa spank terrifically."

"Aw, you make me sick," said Pringle, getting up in disgust. "I don't care whether you believe it or not, you old piece of cheese!"

Tom smiled at the other's retreating form and then looked across the diamond to where Wattles, the very picture of dignity, sat beside Loring with a hand laid precisely on each knee and his back as straight as a ramrod. "Oh, Wattles, how could you!" murmured Tom delightedly. "If I'd only been there to cheer you on!"

Of course Tom confided the news to Clif as soon as the game was over, and after supper they hurried to Loring's room to share the glad tidings. Fortunately Wattles had gone off with Loring's supper tray, and, watching the door apprehensively, Tom related the yarn told by Pringle. Loring's eyes grew round and a wide smile spread over his face as he listened. And finally: "It's absolutely right!" he declared ecstatically.

"You mean you knew about it?" demanded Tom disappointedly.

"No, but when Wattles came back Saturday afternoon, about an hour after I did, he looked mighty funny. He looked—well, I don't know just how he looked, Tom, but sort of like the cat after he'd eaten the canary. He had a lot of red in his cheeks and a kind of—of unholy gleam in his eyes, and he was flustered. Got in his own way and fell over things and was all fussed up about something. And every now and then I'd see him doing this to one of his fingers; sort of working it around and pulling at it, you know. I didn't think much about it, but I did ask him if he'd hurt his hand, and he acted sort of confused and said: 'No, sir' first and then 'Yes, sir,' and finally said that he'd struck it against something and kind of numbed it. But he didn't supply any particulars. Of course what did happen is that he hurt that finger trying to catch a ball! What do you know about Wattles falling for the national pastime, fellows?"

"Shows he's human," said Clif. "I'd like to have seen him, though."

"I'd give a lot to see him," sighed Tom. "I guess what started him was catching that foul the other day. That and reading those 'How to Play Baseball' books you've had around here."

"That was just it," mused Loring, his eyes dancing. "Listen, Tom, do you know what I think? Well, I think that Wattles has made up his mind to be a Big League player! Honest I do. The other evening while he was giving me my rub he said, 'Mr. Loring, is it a fact that professional baseball players receive immense salaries?' I told him it was and asked what he had on his mind, and it seemed that he'd been reading one of those books over there and had come across something about one player getting twenty thousand dollars a year, or some such figure. After that he asked if baseball was something one had to learn in one's youth, and I told him it certainly was. He was very subdued after that. I suspect I discouraged him. But maybe he's got over it now and is starting on his career!"

"Well," laughed Clif, "what I want to know is do we dare josh him. Fact is, Loring, I find our friend Wattles a bit aweing, and I don't suppose I'd have the courage to—"

"For the love of limes," protested Tom, "don't spoil it by letting him know we're on! If we make fun of him he's sure to quit. Keep mum, I say, and some day we'll have a chance of seeing him in action. After that I shan't care what Fate hands me, fellows. I shall have had my Great Moment."

"I guess Tom's right," said Loring to Clif. "I dare say Wattles is getting quite a kick out of it, and it would be a low-down trick to spoil his fun. He's a good sort, old Wattles."

"None better," agreed Tom feelingly. "Gentlemen, a toast! I give you Wattles and His Majesty the King!"

Loring laughed, but he said: "Wattles wouldn't appreciate that joke, Tom. He wants you to thoroughly understand that he's an American. He's the only one I ever heard of who can recite the Declaration of Independence and make you weep!"

They discussed Mr. Cooper's absence presently, Tom pessimistically offering his theory to the effect that the entertaining gentleman had gone his way. "He never did say why he was here or how long he meant to stay," said Tom. "I guess he got bored and beat it back to civilization—or Timbuctoo."

"He wouldn't go without saying good-by to us," declared Loring firmly. "Probably he's just off for a few days. He's bound to show up again."

"Well, if he doesn't, what of it?" asked Tom. "He's all right, but we'd manage somehow without him, I guess."

"He may be sick or something," suggested Clif. "How would it do to 'phone over to the Inn and find out if he's still there?"

"Oh, forget it," said Tom. "You fellows take on about that guy as if he was a long-lost uncle or something. What's the idea? Heck, you don't even know who he is. For all you know he may be a bootlegger or a—a confidence man!"

"Oh, come on down, Tom! You know you like him just as well as Loring and I do. If he's a confidence man you're Babe Ruth!"

"Is that *so*? Well, let me tell you that I may not be batting as well as Babe Ruth does just now, but I'm right after that guy. Yes, sir! And the last picture I saw of him showed him looking mighty worried, too!"

The subject of Mr. Cooper was not revived that evening, and the plan of telephoning to the Inn was not pursued. But the next morning Tom made a visit to the Inn.

He didn't start out for the Inn; or at least that is what he told himself. Having an hour between classes, he decided to take a walk; and what could be more natural than turning his steps toward the village rather than toward the country? It was a partly cloudy morning, warm and damp; there had been several days of just such weather. Spring was in full command now and trees were leaved and meadows were green. Tom didn't walk very fast. It was the time of year, and the sort of day in that time of year, when a fellow doesn't hurry unless he has to. And Tom didn't have to. He was just out to get the air. He might go all the way to the village or he might not. Perhaps he'd only go as far as the Inn before turning back.

When he had reached the Inn he told himself that, since he still had forty-odd minutes to waste, just to prove to the others that he was right about Mr. Cooper he would stop in and inquire at the desk. Of course, way down deep somewhere Tom knew perfectly well that ever since he had got out of bed that morning he had intended to go to the Inn and discover what had become of Mr. Cooper, but it pleased him to pretend that the call was unpremeditated.

"Mr. Cooper?" asked the clerk. "Yes, sir, I think you'll find him in his room, Number 4. Do you know where it is?"

"I can find it, I guess." Tom turned toward the stairway and ascended. The Inn held only half a dozen sleeping rooms and so Number 4 was not far to seek. Outside the closed door, however, Tom hesitated. The fact that Mr. Cooper was still in town and hadn't been around to see them for several days might very easily mean that he had tired of their society, and in that case—

But having come thus far, Tom decided to go through with the business, and knocked. There was an instant response and he went in. Mr. Cooper, wearing a rather dingy dressing robe, was sitting by an open window, and had evidently been reading. At sight of the visitor, however, he dropped his book and got to his feet; not, it seemed, without an effort. "Tom!" he exclaimed with such evident pleasure that the boy's suspicions fled on the instant. He came forward limpingly to rest his one hand on the table and extend the other to the visitor. "Why— By jove, this is awfully decent of you!" The pleasure expressed by voice, look and hearty handclasp left Tom tongue-tied, vaguely embarrassed; and the feeling of embarrassment was not decreased by the sudden knowledge that he was sharing the other's delight to a surprising extent. Mr. Cooper pulled a chair forward and went back to his own seat.

"Well, how are you?" he asked. "I haven't seen any of you for a long while. By the way, I hope you didn't mind my calling you Tom. Surprise rather got the better of formality."

Tom smiled and shook his head. "It's all right with me, sir. I'm fine. We all are, only we were wondering last night why—that is what had become of you. You haven't been ill, sir?"

"Oh, no, it's just this leg. It has a mean way of getting stiff in damp weather. It's better today, though, and I was expecting to get around to watch practice this afternoon."

"Rheumatism, sir?" asked Tom.

"I fancy so. Something of the sort. I got a piece of shrapnel in it about seven years ago, and it's been cranky ever since. Well, how is the Triumvirate getting along? And how are you—er—hitting them?"

Tom answered both questions fully, dwelling at some length on his batting. "I followed your advice, Mr. Cooper," he explained. "You know, you said I wasn't to think about what I was going to do, but just go ahead and do it. Well, that's what I did. I really think I've got the knack of it now, and I'm sure hitting them, sir! You'll see this afternoon."

The visit lasted only a little more than half an hour, but in that time Tom managed to do most of the talking, encouraged by his host, and to confide a good deal of his private history. For instance, Mr. Cooper learned that Tom's mother was dead and that a certain Mr. Winslow was his guardian; that Mr. Winslow was a "pill" in Tom's estimation and that as soon as the latter had finished school he was going to get away; probably enter the Navy, although he might be an explorer instead. "You see," said Tom, "I like to move around and see places. I mean I *would* like to. I never have much, not since I can remember. It must be great to travel around like you do, sir. Gosh, I'd like that! India and China and Africa and everywhere!" Doubtless Mr. Cooper inferred that Tom's father, too, was dead. At least, Tom made no mention of him. Returning to school, Tom's pace was accelerated by two things: a certain excitement generated by the recent conversation and the fact that his next recitation was due in four minutes. Rather oddly, it didn't occur to him that he had been unusually confiding in telling to an acquaintance of a few weeks things he had not revealed to Clif until he had known that youth six months. It had seemed, somehow, very easy, very natural to talk to Mr. Cooper.

He didn't speak to Clif or Loring of his call at the Inn, but Mr. Cooper alluded to it that evening when, bearing somewhat heavily on his cane, he paid his after supper visit to East Hall, and Tom was made to feel the weight of his friends' displeasure. But he didn't seem to mind it. He was in very good spirits tonight.

Perhaps he had a right to be. For one thing, he had been promoted to the first team.

CHAPTER XIV
INSIDE STUFF

THE FIRST HADN'T BEEN getting along very well of late. It had lost to Greenville, won from Cupples and then, last Saturday, had been again defeated, at Clear Lake, by Peebles School. Peebles was not considered strong, yet Wyndham had made but six scattered hits during the contest and had failed to score a run. And Peebles had tallied thrice in the early innings, off Moore, and had fairly walloped Jeff Ogden in the eighth and added four more runs. The Wyndham infield had cracked wide open in that fatal eighth. Coles had accumulated two errors and Tyson and Leland one each. But it was in batting that Wyndham was showing up weakest, and no amount of switching about of the players on the batting order seemed to remedy the weakness. Perhaps Coach Connover took Tom over to the first as a mere gesture of threat, thinking that Tom's presence on the bench might induce Wink Coles and Pat Tyson to greater efforts, for Tom had been performing in very good style on the second and it had occurred to others beside Steve that he might very well be fitted into the first team's infield. Tom's batting was no longer a joke, for he had recently been hitting hard and clean, and, having found himself, might be expected to improve. Then, too, he had the habit of getting to first even when he didn't hit safely. In practice games he was a thorn in the side of Sam Erlingby, working that twirler for pass after pass even in the days when he was notoriously weak at the bat. Once on first, Tom had speed and a certain daring that usually carried him around. At fielding he had become easily the second's star sackman, covering a surprising amount of ground, trying for anything and everything and, in the words of the disgruntled and deposed Evans, "getting away with murder."

Tom joined the big team on Tuesday and replaced Coles for the last three innings of a slow, poorly played contest with the second. On the whole, he was disappointing that day, but he had an alibi in the fact that he was in strange company. He did hit a single that accounted for two runs for his side, however. On Wednesday he saw the Toll's Academy game from the bench. Wyndham experienced a good deal of difficulty in losing that game, but she finally managed it in the ninth when, after carrying it along from the fifth at 5 to 5, Sam Erlingby grooved a ball to the Toll's batsman with two out. Sam had two strikes and two balls on the enemy, and he meant that fast one for a third strike. But the batter laid against it hard and landed it beyond the center of the gridiron and went to third. Even then the game might have gone to extra innings, but Coles, who took the throw-in from Al Greene, thought he saw a chance of nailing the runner at third and made a hurried peg. Perhaps Tyson might have tried harder for that ball, but—well, anyway, it went over his head and the Toll's runner ambled home, and the score was no longer tied. Steve sent in two pinch hitters in the last half, but, although Risley poked out a two bagger and eventually reached third on Greene's out at first, nothing came of it.

On Thursday Tom played second in practice and in the seven-inning game, batting fifth in the list. If he had experienced diffidence on Tuesday he was bravely over it today. To the surprise of his former teammates he appeared not only self-possessed but even self-assured. Getting into fast company seemed to be what he needed. He set a fast pace, and even Hurry Leland was forced to hustle more than once to keep up with him. The first won by a wide margin that afternoon, and while it would be absurd to say that Tom's presence accomplished the victory yet it is certain that it contributed generously to that result. Tom was at the starter's end of two double plays, fielded his position without an error, made a spectacular catch of a short fly well behind first base and, when Greene and Tyson were on second and third with two out, brought in two runs with a smashing hit through the box that Billy Purdy knew enough to let well alone. On the whole Tom spent a busy, pleasant and profitable afternoon; profitable because it won him beyond the shadow of a doubt the right to the position of second base on the first.

"Now," said Loring triumphantly that evening, "now I guess you'll admit that there's something in will power!"

"Well, maybe," answered Tom cautiously. "But tell me this. You knew mighty well that Clif's a better willer than I am. How come, then, that I made the first and he didn't? Run that down!"

"Easy," said Loring. "You started with an advantage. Clif hasn't played as much as you have; before this spring I mean. He probably won't make the first for another week. Maybe two."

Mr. Cooper chuckled and Clif laughed loudly. "You mean two years," said the latter. "I've got as much chance—"

"Hold on!" warned Loring. "That's the wrong thought, Clif. Just remember this. When we started this—this campaign neither you nor Tom had much idea of even making the second. Now Tom's gone up to the first and you've licked Burke for center fielder. There's three weeks yet, and if we all carry on and concentrate hard—"

"And play hard," interpolated Mr. Cooper quietly.

"Yes, and play hard, there's no telling what may happen. Mr. Connover still needs fellows on his team who can make hits, Clif, and if you keep on swatting the way you have been, and we all put our thoughts on it, I wouldn't be surprised if Mr. Connover took you over, too."

Clif stared incredulously. "You're nutty, Loring," he sighed. "It's a shame, too, for you gave promise of becoming a brilliant guy some day. I guess you're one of those—those monomaniacs you read about."

"Seems to me," observed Tom, "you and Steve are getting sort of thick, Loring. It looked this afternoon as if you were telling him how to run the team."

"Not exactly," laughed Loring, "but we were having a rather hot argument."

"For Pete's sake! What about?"

"Oh, I don't mean a violent argument. Perhaps discussion would be better. You remember when first had Raiford on third and Talbott on second with two out in the fourth inning? The second team infield played back to get the runner at first base. Well, Mr. Connover told Cobham to hit it out. His thought was, of course, that if Cob hit safely those two runs would come across. What Cob did do was fly out to Slim Scott about ten feet back of the base path. I wanted to get at Mr. Connover's reasoning and so I asked him. He told me that Cob was ordinarily a long hitter, when he did hit, and that as those two runs were badly needed he thought the best play was to let Cob soak the ball."

"And why wasn't it?" asked Clif. "Cob has got some long hits off Purdy before today."

"Perhaps it was," answered Loring. "But it didn't seem so to me. That's what led to the discussion."

"You think Cob should have bunted, eh?" asked Tom.

"Yes, because the infielders were playing too far back to handle a bunt to first base in time. Cob's a left-handed batter. If he had laid a bunt down the first base line Raiford would have scored, Talbott would have reached third and Cob would have been safe."

"And there'd have been one run in instead of two," objected Tom.

"But still only two down. Cob could have stolen second on the first pitch, and the situation would have been just as it was before, except that the infield might have played short, expecting the next man would also bunt, and in that case any sort of a hit past the infield would have scored again. What really happened—"

"Sure. Cob flied out because he picked a bad one," said Tom. "But if he had hit safe—"

"Oh, I know it all depends on the 'ifs,'" laughed Loring, "but I still think the situation called for a bunt."

"Well, but Billy wasn't pitching high ones, maybe, and not one fellow in twenty can bunt a low delivery."

"But Billy *was* pitching high ones," said Loring. "He was putting them over the corners, or trying to, just under Cob's arms. He wanted Cob to hit the ball on the ground."

"But," asked Tom, "how the dickens was Steve to know beforehand that Billy would pitch 'em high?"

"Perhaps he couldn't have known, but he might have guessed that Billy wouldn't feed low ones, because Cob likes that kind and might easily have sent a long fly into the outfield where it couldn't have been handled. If I'd been Cobham I'd have done this, Tom. I'd have waited for a couple of deliveries to see what the pitcher had on his mind. Then if he was offering high ones I'd have bunted, or tried to. If I saw he wasn't going to let me bunt I'd have faked a bunt in hopes that the infield would come in at least halfway. If it did I'd have tried to drop a hit just behind it."

"Help!" exclaimed Tom. "The old bean's getting groggy, son! Say, where'd you get all this inside stuff? Not just reading those books?"

"Well, I suppose I've got some of my theories from the books and some from watching play. Probably I'm cheeky to put out such a line, considering I've never played. It's a wonder Coach didn't tell me to shut up, but he didn't. He argued it out just as though I had some sense. He was mighty decent."

"Well," asked Mr. Cooper interestedly, "how was it decided?"

"It wasn't," laughed Loring. "Six rounds, no decision."

"At that," said Tom reflectively, "I think you were right, old son. Cob's a pretty good bunter. Of course, the bunt might have gone foul or been too hard or—"

"Or Cob might have stubbed his toe," interrupted Clif. "You don't either of you know what you're talking about. I'm for Loring keeping out of it and letting Steve run his gang the way he thinks best so we can continue to beat you fellows, Tom, two or three times a week, for the good of your souls."

The first went to Wessex two days later and played Broadmoor, and while they were once more defeated, they won honor nevertheless. The final score, reached in the twelfth inning, was 9 to 8. Good pitching by both sides, clean fielding and bunched hits were the rule, and Wyndham's final overthrow was entirely a one-man result.

A pass in the last half of the twelfth put a Broadmoor runner on first. A strike-out followed and then Cobham's throw to Captain Leland, covering second, was just wide enough to allow the runner to slide into the bag. The incident perhaps unsteadied Ogden, for he slid his next offering along the groove and it found the bat in front of it. The ball went toward center field and fell in No Man's Land. Al Greene ran in and Tom ran out, and the ball landed between them, a half-dozen strides from Al. The runner, chancing a double play for the sake of a winning tally, had sped away from second while the ball was still in air, and when Greene scooped the ball from the ground was already rounding third. Al performed a bit of quick reasoning then that cost his team the game. He decided that the runner was bluffing and had no real intention of going on to the plate. If so a fast throw to third might catch him before he could double back. So Al threw to Tyson. It was a good heave and reached Pat on a straight, fast bound, and had the runner meant to play safe and wait on third for a hit to get home on he might have been tagged out. But by the time Tyson had the ball in his hands the runner, who had not even hesitated at the corner sack, was hitting the homestretch. Pat's peg was a bit high, and by the time Cobham had caught, taken one stride and swept his hand down the runner was scraping a dusty shoe across the rubber and Broadmoor was shouting jubilantly.

Disappointment lasted but a short time, however, for, all in all, Wyndham had played a better game from every angle than she had played all season. Manager Longwell exhibited the score book, and that told the tale. Al Greene was disconsolate for a space but found comfort in the fact that the error column held no figures opposite his name. Fortunately, perhaps, errors of judgment do not find their way into the box scores.

CHAPTER XV
WATTLES IS CARELESS

THE BROADMOOR GAME BROUGHT the first week of June to an end. Extremely warm weather held New England, and warm weather, as usual, produced a let-up of scholastic ambition in many cases. Tom, for one, found studying more difficult than ever, and for the third time that year received a grave warning from Mr. Wyatt, the English teacher. Remembering only too well what had occurred on one previous occasion, Tom braced up for several days and, with many protests and groans, labored back into Alick's good graces. But it required the assistance and encouragement of Clif and Loring to get him there, and it was the Triumvirate rather than Tom who succeeded. With final examinations impending, it was no time, as Loring pointed out, to get penalized.

Loring was getting a great deal of enjoyment out of life those days. That discussion with Coach Connover had led to others. Steve, although he was perhaps never swayed by Loring's views, seemed to find the boy's theories and judgments interesting. It was at his suggestion that Loring's chair was rolled to the end of the players' bench of an afternoon, and frequently the coach slipped into the seat beside him and conversed. He was genuinely surprised when Loring confessed to having witnessed but four baseball games previous to this spring and to having obtained what knowledge of the game he possessed from the perusal of every book on the subject that he had been able to lay hands on and from watching the practice. In defense Loring said one day:

"Of course, Mr. Connover, I understand that I don't really know much about the game. A fellow can't, I guess, unless he plays it. All I've got is a lot of theoretical stuff. It—it's mighty good of you not to laugh at me, sir."

"Laugh at you? Nonsense, Deane. What you call theoretical stuff is perfectly sound, and I find it remarkable that you have absorbed so much of it without—how shall I put it?—without more incentive. Here you are, physically barred from playing, with a full knowledge of baseball, and all around us are fellows actually engaged in playing who don't know the rules of the game, to say nothing of the strategy. No, you don't owe anyone an apology for being able to talk baseball intelligently, Deane, and if I don't always agree with you it isn't because your theories are wrong but because no theory—no baseball theory, at least—is always applicable in practice. A certain situation may call for one procedure today and a different procedure tomorrow, and that is largely because theories do not take into consideration the personal equation. I am not, of course, speaking now of the few hard and fast—er—tenets of the game; laws firmly established by experience; but of the more hypothetical theories that we call 'inside stuff.' Given a certain situation, Deane, the coach or the captain has to measure the book theory against all sorts of conditions; the opposing team's reactions to certain moves, the abilities of his own players to perform those moves, many things. A play that might succeed in the early innings would fail in the later for any one of a number of reasons. Even weather is a factor, and as for psychology—" Steve sighed—"once a coach starts on psychology he's lost!"

"I'm afraid I don't understand that," said Loring.

"Well, what I meant is that it's so plaguy easy to overdo that part of it, Deane, so easy to let psychology take the place of common sense. Besides, what does anyone know about it, after all? As a practical aid to winning ball games it's been a good deal overrated, I think. Baseball writers like to use the phrase 'the psychology of the game,' but more than likely what they call a psychological manifestation—or whatever they *do* call it—if tracked down will resolve into some such chance happening as a ball hitting a pebble and bounding wrong or a pitcher having a twinge in his elbow as he lets the ball go. All the psychology in the world won't win a ball game, Deane, or lose one; not unless we call psychology by a shorter name."

"You mean—luck, sir?"

"Chance," said Mr. Connover. "Chance, the finest baseball and football general in the histories of the games!"

Wattles, seated slightly behind the wheelchair, listened in rapt attention to the talks and discussions. There were times during a debate on the proper play with which to meet a situation when Wattles allowed himself a slight compression of the lips or a faintly eloquent elevation of the eyebrows. Occasionally Wattles might express agreement of a hearty character by placing an immaculate handkerchief to his nose and trumpeting loudly. But he knew his place, did Wattles, and no matter how vehemently he might agree or disagree with the contentions of either the coach or Loring he kept his mouth tight. Perhaps it was not easy, either, for Wattles, too, had delved into baseball lore, reading word for word with Loring, and had formed opinions. Then, too, Wattles had one advantage over Loring. Wattles had played the game!

He had never mentioned that lapse from dignity, nor had Loring ever questioned. Wattles had had more than thirty minutes of thrills that Saturday afternoon when, jokingly invited by the boy who clerked in Burger's drug store, he had cast discretion to the winds, removed part of his apparel and chased about over a dusty field in pursuit of an elusive ball. Afterwards he had regretted the affair. Or had he? He was never quite certain as to that. Certain it was, however, that the memory of those wild moments still brought a glow; and certain it was, although Wattles sternly refused to acknowledge it, that if a like opportunity occurred again he would once more forget his dignity and his derby!

The first team was now down to seventeen members, its roster including Ogden, Moore, Erlingby and Frost, pitchers; Cobham and Risley, catchers; Van Dyke, Kemble, Tyson, Leland, Coles and Jackson, infielders; Raiford, Greene, Talbott, Pierce and Lester, outfielders. Two or three players who had survived the middle of the season had gone to the second, displacing others or, after a brief test, retiring to private life. The second kept sixteen men. On the Saturday afternoon that the first had journeyed away to play Broadmoor the second had met Freeburg High School in the first contest of its three game schedule with outside teams and had met with a sound drubbing. The second was woefully weak in its pitching department, and the opponent had batted Purdy from the mound in the fourth inning and treated his successor no more kindly. The only thing that prevented Coach Wadleigh from putting in a third twirler in the seventh was the fact that there wasn't any third. Clif had a busy afternoon, running after balls until he quite lost his breath in the seventh inning. He had six chances during the engagement and accepted them all. If he could have done as well at bat he would have completed a very satisfactory day's work, but he didn't have much luck against the High School pitcher, getting but one hit, a two-bagger. The other three times at the plate he struck out. Some of his companions saw nothing deceptive in the pitcher's offerings and found them frequently, but he remained an enigma to Clif all through the game except in the third when the latter managed to connect with a fast one. Freeburg won in the end by the lop-sided score of 11 to 4.

During practice these days Clif was utterly deserted by his fellow members of the Triumvirate, for Tom had long since departed to the other diamond and now Loring, facetiously termed by Clif the Advisory Council, spent his afternoons hobnobbing with Coach Connover. Even Mr. Cooper's lean brown face was no longer to be seen above the rail of the first base stand, for he, too, had found the attractions of the big team superior. Or perhaps it was his interest in Tom which caused him to desert his old friends, for there was no blinking the fact that he and Tom were getting to be as thick as thieves. Clif resented that a little. It really didn't make a bit of difference in the relations between Tom and him, for the companionship Mr. Cooper offered was that of an older person and didn't in the least endanger Tom's regard for Clif, but the latter couldn't help feeling a trifle jealous at times. Why, it had got so of late that Tom went over to the Inn three or four mornings a week! Clif didn't like Mr. Cooper any the less, however; indeed, those pangs of resentment were neither frequent nor profound, and he did his best to discourage them. Bit by bit they were learning more of Mr. Cooper. They knew now that he had served in the English Army during the War, had been invalided twice, once for wounds and once for gassing, and had been discharged with the rank of lieutenant. This information came from Tom and was the result of his visits to the Inn. Tom declared, also, that he was plumb certain Mr. Cooper had all sorts of decorations, although he had neither heard of nor seen any of them. As an indication of how the gentleman stood with Loring and Clif, it may be mentioned that neither of them doubted for a moment that Tom was correct in his surmise.

Mr. Cooper had made other friends and acquaintances beside the members of the Triumvirate and had become a familiar figure about the school. Mr. Clendennin, head of the Junior School, and "Lovey" McKnight, who was the chemistry instructor and, incidentally, Clif's advisor, were among Mr. Cooper's growing circle of intimates, while, to the surprise of the Triumvirate, he was discovered by them one evening at supper with Doctor Wyatt. That in itself was not so astounding, since "J. W." frequently acted as host to school visitors, but the fact that Mr. Cooper had made no mention of the incident to them and went through with it so casually perplexed the boys. Later, apprised by Tom that he had been seen in dining hall, he merely said: "Oh, really? I thought the food remarkably good."

Curiosity prompted Clif to seek information of Mr. McKnight one evening, and so, after the instructor's opinion had been obtained on a matter regarding the approaching examinations, Clif introduced the subject of Mr. Cooper. "You know, sir, we like him a lot," said Clif. "It's funny, but he doesn't seem much older than we are. I mean he isn't—isn't stodgy a bit; doesn't try to make a chap realize that he's just a kid and doesn't know much of anything. You know, some men *are* like that!"

The last sentence was added defensively in response to Lovey's smile.

"Yes, I guess they are," Lovey agreed. "And I can easily see that Cooper wouldn't be. I found him very interesting and likable, too, Clif."

"Yes, sir." Clif hesitated. "He didn't tell you— I mean, you don't happen to know why he's here, sir?"

"Here? In Freeburg? Why, no, he didn't say. And I didn't ask him. In fact, it didn't occur to me, Clif. But why shouldn't he be here?"

"I suppose there isn't any reason why he shouldn't," laughed Clif, "only it seems sort of a dead place to *live* in. I mean to say, if you hadn't some *reason* for doing it, sir, you wouldn't hit on this place as a—a residence, now would you?"

"I wouldn't," agreed the instructor, "but another man might. I could imagine a chap who was looking for the quiet life in an attractive village being quite satisfied with Freeburg. The Inn isn't so bad, Clif, and you've got to own that this part of the country is mighty pretty in spring. Perhaps Mr. Cooper is doing some writing or—well, reading. I understand there are still a few in this country who sometimes read."

"I don't think it's that, though," pondered Clif. "Tom goes to see him pretty often, sir, and he says Mr. Cooper hasn't many books in his room. Awhile ago he borrowed one from Loring Deane, a book on baseball."

"Well, he will doubtless tell us if he wants us to know, Clif. After all," he added with a twinkle, "it's rather more his affair than ours."

"Yes, of course," Clif flushed slightly. "I guess you think I'm sort of cheeky, sir, but—"

"No," Mr. McKnight laughed, "I just think that you're a whole lot like the rest of us, Clif; that is, extremely curious about things that don't really concern us. That is a lamentable feature, old chap, of our national character."

So Clif departed better informed on the national character, but with no new information regarding Mr. Cooper.

Yet new information was forthcoming. From Mr. McKnight's study in West Hall Clif made his way, through the dim corridor of Middle, to East and down the stairs to Loring's room on the first floor. Mr. Cooper, Tom, Loring and Wattles were on hand when he entered in the middle of a debate on Wyndham's chance to win from Horner Academy in the boat races to be held a few days later. Wattles, of course, was not taking part in the discussion, being busy in a corner of the room with a bottle of odorless cleanser and a couple of dozen of Loring's neckties, but he looked as if ready to supply an opinion if it was asked for. Wattles in the past eight months had become an ardent Wyndhamian and was firmly convinced that the Dark Blue could whip anything on land or water; or, discounting the future, in the air, for that matter!

This was an election year, and the newspapers were giving much space to the impending national conventions. Loring was greatly interested in politics, a subject which bored Tom supremely, and after the boat races had been exhausted Loring asked: "Who are you going to vote for for President, Mr. Cooper?"

Mr. Cooper smiled a little. "I can tell you which of the candidates I fancy I'd vote for if I were going to vote," he replied.

"If you were going— But do you mean that you aren't, sir?" Loring sounded outraged. "Why, don't you think that every citizen—"

"Absolutely, Loring! But, you see, I'm not a citizen."

"How do you mean, sir?" asked Tom.

"I mean that I'm not an American citizen. I thought you chaps knew."

"Why, no, sir!" exclaimed Tom. "I thought of course you were. Heck, that's a blow! May I ask why you aren't? I mean, what—"

Mr. Cooper chuckled. "I was born in Derbyshire, England, Tom. And although I've lived over here a good part of my life, and in other countries another good part, I'm still a subject of His Majesty King George."

There was a suppressed exclamation from Wattles in the corner of the room, followed by the thud of the bottle of cleansing fluid against the carpet and the *glug-glug* of its wasting contents.

CHAPTER XVI
A DOUBLE DEFEAT

HIGHLAND SCHOOL WAS DEFEATED, 6 to 4, at Highland, on Wednesday, in a loosely played game in which errors on both sides accounted for most of the tallies. Frost was in the box for Wyndham and might have stayed through the whole contest had he had good backing. As it was, miscues in the sixth inning let in three Highland runs, and Frosty got wobbly and was relieved by Erlingby. Tom helped pile up the Dark Blue's total of three errors, contributing an unfortunate fumble which, like most of his errors, was due to over-eagerness. Highland got no more tallies after Erlingby's arrival on the mound, and, in the eighth, Wyndham combined a hit, a sacrifice and a stolen base with a Highland error and put two more runs across, bringing the score to 6 to 4, at which it remained. Catcher Cobham emerged from the battle with a split finger on his throwing hand, an injury destined to keep him out of baseball for nearly two weeks. Gus Risley, who had taken Cob's place in the seventh inning, was a far less dependable backstop although a distinct addition to the batting strength of the team.

On Saturday Horner Academy came over from across the New York border to prove her superiority in both rowing and baseball. The enemy's colors were so much in evidence that forenoon that Freeburg took on a most festive appearance. Everyone who could went over to the lake shortly after noon and witnessed the visitor capture the lion's share of the water contest. Loring's father and mother arrived in the car, and he and Wattles and one of the Junior School boys motored over. Mr. Bingham also came up that morning, unexpectedly, and filled his car with Clif, Walter Treat and three others. Tom couldn't go, for the first team players were to have an hour's practice before the game.

The junior eight's contest was held first, and once more the second crew showed their gameness. In spite of their showing against Highland, they were not looked on as winners today, and so it was a distinct surprise when the dark blue oars flashed into the lead at the start, held the lead to the quarter flag, lost it just beyond, though by no more than a few yards, and recovered it before the half-way marker. That was a pretty race all the way, for, while

Wyndham was never headed, Horner rowed desperately and was no more than a boat's length behind when the final quarter began. For a space a gallant rally carried her to almost even terms, but Wyndham also hit up her stroke and maintained it to the line, something Horner was incapable of, and shot across, to the shrieks of her adherents, not quite two lengths ahead.

Wyndham accepted that result as a good augury for the big event, but the latter, which started at two-thirty, proved a reversal of fortune. It was Horner who got away to a fine start this time and Wyndham who trailed all the way to the finish. Billy Desmond and his seven companions in the Dark Blue's shell rowed themselves out before the distance was three-fourths covered, went on heroically but raggedly and fairly collapsed with the coxswain's shout of "Let her run!" Horner had showed a generous six lengths of water behind her boat at the finish.

Wyndham had to be satisfied with the minor victory of the junior eight as she hustled back to school for the ball game. Mr. Cooper joined Clif and his father and Walter Treat and the quartet witnessed this contest from seats behind third base. Mr. Cooper and Mr. Bingham, it must be acknowledged, failed to manifest unflagging interest. They seemed to find a number of subjects more interesting than baseball, and there were moments when Clif was rather impatient with his father because the latter allowed his attention to wander. Walter was a nice chap, and Clif liked him a lot, but Walter was no baseball fan and displayed at times the crassest ignorance.

The game was well played and almost every inning supplied a thrill, but after the fourth frame only the most optimistic of Wyndham rooters dared predict a victory for the home team. The Wyndham infield was playing together like a well-oiled machine, Jeff Ogden was holding the visitors to a few scattered hits and Fortune remained impartial. But while Horner had failed during four innings to get a man as far as third base, Wyndham had failed to get one to first! It was plain enough to be seen that Horner's aggressive batters were destined to come into their own ultimately, and when that happened the boy at the score board was going to stop hanging up goose eggs!

It happened in the first half of the fifth inning. The Horner shortstop, second man on the list, hit safely past Captain Leland and went to second on a sacrifice out, Tom to Van Dyke. The visitor's third baseman fell on one of Ogden's curves and poled out a two-bagger into left field, scoring the first run of the game. Hurry handled the next out, an easy grounder, throwing to first. A sharp liner through the box scored the second tally. On an attempted steal the last hitter was pegged out at second by Risley.

For Wyndham, Raiford fouled out to third baseman, Tom flied out to first and Talbott fanned. There was no more scoring until the eighth. Then Horner sent her third tally over the plate on a hit, a sacrifice and a long fly-out to left fielder. Yet every inning between had seen men on bases and runs apparently imminent. Even Wyndham revived the hopes of her supporters in the seventh by getting Tyson as far as third on a scratch hit, a sacrifice bunt by Captain Leland and an out. Risley went to bat amidst loud acclaim. Clif, red-faced from recent vocal exertions, begged Gus to "make it a homer!" But the best the substitute catcher could do was arch a tremendously long fly into the outfield where, having been warned of Risley's batting prowess, the Horner center fielder was playing well back toward the running track and had only to step a few yards to his left to make the catch.

Horner failed to threaten in the first half of the ninth, and Wyndham went to bat with the Blue's adherents imploring a victory. But although Tom started things going, after Raiford had fouled out, with a hot liner through shortstop's legs and got to second when Talbott hit along the base path and was safe when the baseman juggled the hurried throw, nothing came of the rally. Van Dyke struck out, and Jackson, batting for Jeff Ogden, lifted a high fly to shortstop, and the game was over, the score 3 to 0.

Wyndham had played an errorless game, had made five hits and had been defeated. Horner had made two errors, batted safely ten times and had won. From which it was fairly adjudged by a somewhat indignant student body that what the home team needed were a few fellows who could hit the pellet! That was also the decision arrived at that evening when Mr. Bingham and Mr. Cooper played hosts to the Triumvirate at the Inn. Tom, who had made one of the Wyndham hits, attempted a rather vague excuse for the first team but was squelched by Clif and Loring. He finally confessed that something ought to be done, adding brightly: "We might put our thoughts on 'em, Loring. Maybe we could will a bunch of bingles the next time, eh? What price psychology?"

Clif begged him not to be a giddy ass.

"I don't suppose," acknowledged Loring, "that it's quite practical to work mental suggestion on a whole baseball team but we might pick out a few of the worst batters and try it on them."

The idea seemed to amuse Mr. Bingham immensely, and he chuckled and chuckled over it, the glowing end of his cigar waggling up and down in the darkness of the porch. Clif said, almost accusingly: "I don't see that psychology has done me a whole lot of good. I'm still on the scrub!"

"But," responded Tom gently, "think where you'd be without it! Playing with the West Hall Terriers, probably."

"I didn't know that you were keen about promotion," said Mr. Bingham. "Thought you were doing pretty well where you are and quite satisfied, son."

"Oh, well," said Clif, "I'd rather make the first, of course. Any fellow would, I guess. Besides, if Tom gets on I don't see why I can't. Everyone knows I'm far superior to him."

"My Sainted Aunt Jerusha!" breathed Tom in awe. "Hear that boy talk! Mr. Bingham, I used to be known as 'the King of the Diamond' when Clif was in rompers!"

"Let's see," chuckled Mr. Bingham, "what's the difference in your ages, Tom?"

"More than five months," replied Tom impressively.

"In whose favor?" asked Mr. Cooper innocently, and that brought a laugh.

"Anyway," said Tom, returning to gravity, "our gang's got to learn to hit better than it's been hitting before next Saturday or we'll be gone coons. Wolcott's been swatting the old apple hard all the season. Look what she did a week ago Saturday. Got fourteen hits off that Goodwin pitcher, what's-his-name!"

"Deering," said Loring. "But he's nothing much."

"Just the same, we couldn't hit him when we played there during vacation. Well, maybe our fellows did touch him up a bit, but we didn't get anything like fourteen off him, and we lost the game."

"You play Wolcott next Saturday?" asked Mr. Bingham. "Does Wolcott come here, or—"

"Yes, sir," answered Clif. "That's the first game. We go to Cotterville Tuesday for the second and then play here again Wednesday in case of a tie."

"There won't be any game next Wednesday," declared Tom pessimistically. "If we can't hit a poor fish like that fellow who pitched against us today we certainly can't touch that left-hander of theirs, Osterman; or Rice either. Those guys are *good*! And I guess that fast ball artist of theirs isn't much worse."

"I don't believe that Osterman is a bit better than Jeff Ogden," said Loring stoutly. "And here's another thing, Tom. We've got three left-hand pitchers to Wolcott's two."

"What of it? They've got a second-string outfield of left-hand batters!"

"Where do you get all this dope?" asked Clif.

"I read the papers, son. Wolcott had five out of nine fellows in her batting-list hitting left-handed a couple of weeks ago against Brown Prep. Brown put in a left-hand twirler, and Wolcott switched half her gang and punched out enough hits to win. I call that strategy, what?"

"Gosh," said Clif, "the trouble with our team is that there aren't five on it who can hit right-handed, to say nothing of left! Just the same, I'll bet we cop the first game anyway, and if we lose the second we've still got a chance in the third; and playing on your own field, with a lot of fellows cheering you and everyone pulling your way, is bound to help."

"Sure, and we're going to need that help," said Tom grimly. "I wish Steve would change the batting order and see how it would go. Greene isn't any good as a lead-off man. Hurry would be a lot better. If the first fellow up doesn't draw his base one way or another, what good is he? And Al Greene's got his base when he's led off just about once since I joined the team."

"I'd like to see Coach try you there," observed Loring.

"Me?" Tom sounded a trifle startled. "Well, at that I'll bet I'd get my base oftener than Greene does. I may not be any—any—"

"Clouter Hearn," offered Clif.

"Shut up! What I mean is, I—I—well, call it luck if you like—"

"What else could it be?" chuckled Clif.

Tom aimed a kick at him, missed by inches and subsided.

"Well," declared Loring with conviction, "you chaps are going to see a big improvement in our team's hitting next Saturday. You may depend on that."

"Is that *so*?" inquired Tom. "You and Steve have got it all settled, eh? I suppose Miller Huggins is going to loan us Babe Ruth for the afternoon!"

"Maybe, but I haven't heard of it. No, what I mean is just this, Tom. There isn't a fellow on the team who can't hit if he wants to; I mean there isn't one who hasn't the ability to hit. You fellows have got in a slump, that's your trouble. You started out pretty well and went along all right until about the sixth week of the season. It was the Greenville game that started you on the down grade. Ever since then you've been off your game. Including the Greenville game, you've lost five and won two, I think."

"Your statistics are absolutely correct," said Tom, "only I object to the—the inference you suggest."

"What inference?" asked Loring.

"That the blamed old team was getting along all right until I joined it!"

"Facts speak for themselves," said Clif.

"All right, then. Facts narrate that Wyndham won six games, lost three and tied one before she played Greenville. I'm just telling you this to prove that I wasn't the hoodoo. I didn't go to the first until after the Peebles game."

"Since when," remarked Clif maliciously, "we've been licked four times."

"Just how many games have been won and how many lost?" asked Mr. Bingham, lighting a fresh cigar.

"It's pretty bad, Mr. Bingham," said Loring. "We've won eight, lost eight and tied one. If we win all the remaining games we can't finish with better than eleven victories. I remember that Mr. Connover said that first day in the cage, Clif, that he expected the team to win at least fourteen out of twenty-two."

"That was bluff," said Tom. "Coaches always make cracks like that at the start of the season."

"Well, then, what about your enemy?" asked Mr. Bingham. "What has Wolcott been doing?"

"I don't know exactly, sir," Loring replied, "but I think she has won about two-thirds of her schedule so far. Oh, she's made a much better showing than we have, there's no doubt of that!"

"Mustn't think about that," murmured Mr. Cooper. "Always start a scrap with the conviction that you're better than the other chap."

"That's right," agreed Loring; and,

"Yeah, psychology," grunted Tom.

CHAPTER XVII
LORING GOES SCOUTING

MONDAY FOUND THE SCHOOL deep in examinations, with anxious countenances everywhere in evidence. Practice didn't commence until four o'clock, and games with the second were canceled for the rest of the season. The second team played two games that week, one with Granleigh High School on Tuesday, which went to only five innings, and one with Waterside on Thursday. The latter spread over seven good, fast innings and was captured by the home team in the sixth. The Granleigh contest resulted in a 4 to 4 tie. On Wednesday the first played its second game with Freeburg and won it, 8 to 2. There was only time for six innings, but those six showed Wyndham's superiority to the High School and brought back a glimmer of hope to the Dark Blue's supporters. The Freeburg pitchers were not difficult, perhaps, but eleven hits in six frames, even against mediocre twirlers, was held to be encouraging. And with the first Wolcott contest but three days distant a little encouragement went a long way!

Tom was not enjoying himself very much those days. He expressed the conviction, a rather faint conviction, that he would get good enough marks in his studies to pass, but since by Wednesday he had accumulated nothing better than *D*'s his friends weren't so sanguine. "Of course I'll flop in English," he explained resignedly, "but I ought to get a *B* in Hygiene and a *C* in History, and if I do I'll pull through. Anyhow, if I don't I should worry. Old Winslow says I can't come back if I don't pass, and I'm not letting that trouble me, either. I don't believe he has any notion of letting me go to college, so why kill myself getting through here?"

"But you'd rather come back next year than not, I fancy," said Mr. Cooper. They were sitting in the stand while the rest of the team gathered for practice.

"Oh, well, I don't know," replied Tom carelessly. "I guess I'd rather go into the Navy or something. I'd like to see the world, Mr. Cooper."

"Of course, but there'd be time enough after college. Or you could do a bit of travel in summer."

"Swell chance with old Winslow holding the purse strings!"

"Really? But he wouldn't object to your going across now and then, would he?"

"He'd object if I wanted to cross the Hudson River," said Tom. "Oh, I suppose there isn't much money in the old sock. He never will tell me how much I've got. When I ask him he just hems and haws and shakes his head and looks like a dying fish. He seems to think I ought to earn a scholarship. Can't you see me doing it?" Tom grinned at his companion. "His idea is that unless I get swell marks here there's no use in my staying. He's going to throw a fit when he sees what I get in finals!"

"If you fail to pass I dare say you could do a bit of tutoring this summer and get back again, eh?"

"Oh, sure, I could, but— Well, Mr. Cooper, it's like this. I've sort of made up my mind that if I don't pass I'll just take a sneak. Honest, there's not much fun at home in the summer. Mr. Winslow sticks there all through the hot weather, and if I want to go anywhere for more than a day he blame near faints. By gosh, I'd just like to know how much money my mother did leave me!"

"Well, Tom," said Mr. Cooper, tapping the ashes from his pipe, "I'd rather like to see you go through here at Wyndham. I have a fancy that Winslow will—I mean to say that you'll get to college all right, old chap. Fact is, I'd really appreciate it if you'd try real hard to pass these examinations, Tom. Might consider it as a sort of favor to me."

Tom looked a little surprised, but a little pleased, too. He turned his gaze to Pat Tyson, who was doing a juggling act with four baseballs for the benefit of a group of early arrivals down by the bench, and after a moment said: "All right, sir. Sure, I'll do my best, only—only I wouldn't think it would make much difference to you, sir."

"Why not?" asked Mr. Cooper quietly. "You and I— Well, to be frank, Tom, I've got to liking you. Quite a lot. I hope you don't mind me saying that." Mr. Cooper reddened and his voice held embarrassment.

"No, sir, I don't," replied Tom stoutly. He still stared into the diamond, though. "I—I like it." He turned and gave the man a brief glance and then, with a little nervous laugh, added: "It's fifty-fifty, sir."

"Honestly, old chap?" Mr. Cooper's tone was so eager, so pleased, so almost anxious as well, that Tom wondered and felt his own cheeks reddening. He didn't like to be embarrassed. So he only nodded. After a pause Mr. Cooper said: "That's the coach, isn't it?" Rather a silly question when you came to think of it, for Mr. Connover, who was no more than forty paces distant, didn't resemble anyone but himself. But Tom answered: "Yes, sir," seriously enough and pulled himself up preparatory to vaulting the rail. Then, rather diffidently, he said: "Don't you worry about me passing, Mr. Cooper. I'll skin through somehow!"

As usual, Loring had Wattles push his chair to the end of the players' bench, and as usual most of the fellows came to him sooner or later for a word or a chat. His score book, a leather-covered affair, lay on his knees, and a well-sharpened pencil protruded from a pocket. Learning to keep a score correctly was, he had discovered, not so easy, and he was still obliged to call on the official scorer for assistance. Today he meant to go across to the other field after awhile and watch the second team's game with Waterside and fill one more page of his book with neat little figures and symbols. As it turned out, however, he didn't do just that, for by the time the second and its opponent had finished warming up and were ready to begin their delayed struggle Loring found himself in converse with Coach Connover and too interested to leave. Steve never appeared discomposed or even anxious, yet today Loring thought he could detect an undercurrent of concern in the coach's casual discussion of the players and their work. But before that Steve made a suggestion that captured Loring's interest at once.

"Deane, you have two more years here, haven't you?" asked the coach. "I thought so. Well, why don't you compete next year for a manager's job? It's something you could easily attend to, and you'd like it, I know. Better consider it."

"Why, do you think—do you think I could, Mr. Connover?" gasped the boy. "You know I can't get around very—very fast!"

"Fast enough, I guess. You've got executive ability, Deane; plenty of it; which is more than most managers have. Of course, the position of manager or assistant doesn't earn a great deal of glory; you don't stand in the limelight much; but it's a lot more important than most folks believe, and a good manager is worth a lot to his team. Well, I think you could be a good manager, and I'd certainly like to see you try for it. I believe that right now you know a lot more baseball than any of the three fellows who are holding down the jobs this spring."

"Why, thanks," murmured Loring, "but—gee, I don't know! I couldn't be better than an assistant year after next, could I?"

"No, not in the ordinary course of events," was the reply. "But an assistant, if he's capable and has a head on him, is frequently of more real value than the manager himself. In fact, Deane, as you may have noticed, it's the assistants who do most of the work! I wish I'd thought of it before, so you could have competed this year. But I didn't know you so well, you see."

"I'd like awfully to try it," said Loring eagerly. "You see, sir, there isn't very much that I can do here; a fellow has to be able to get around a good deal, of course, if he tries for—for things; but if you think I'd be able to do that, supposing I succeeded in getting by, I'd love to try it."

"Oh, you'd get by, and you'd be able to handle the job when you got it. And it might just happen that for some reason you could land something better than an assistant's job. You never can tell a year ahead what's going to happen. Fellows drop out of school or resign, you know. Think it over, anyhow."

Mr. Connover arose and went out to the pitcher's box, and the practice, which had slowed up in the last few minutes, took on new vigor. Loring remained silent several minutes, thinking over what the coach had said. It would be really wonderful if he could make good Mr. Connover's prediction, if he could be of use in the school. Why, being an assistant baseball manager would be almost like playing the game! He turned suddenly to the silent Wattles.

"Did you hear what Mr. Connover was saying, Wattles?" he asked.

"Yes, sir, perfectly."

"Well, what do you think? Do you believe I could do it?"

"Oh, very easily, sir. The position of manager doesn't strike me, Mr. Loring, as being a very arduous one, although there may be more to it than—er—strikes the eye."

"Well, I do think I could do the—the work," replied Loring. "What I meant was would I—could we get around as we'd have to? Out here every day, and away with the team on its trips, I suppose, and running around to see different fellows. It would take quite a lot of pushing, Wattles!"

"We could do it, sir. I've no doubt the young gentlemen would make it as easy as possible for you, Mr. Loring."

"But that's just it, Wattles. I wouldn't want any favors, and I'm afraid I couldn't—couldn't fill the bill without them."

"I think you could, sir." Wattles became suddenly apprehensively alert as a ball arched into the air behind the catcher, but it descended a good twenty feet away and Wattles relaxed again. "Mr. Loring, I've been thinking for some time that if we had wider tires on the chair it would be a deal better. These are quite satisfactory indoors, sir, but they do go a bit hard on the turf. Now, if you see what I mean, sir, a—er—wider traction—I think traction is the word—"

"It is, Wattles, and I do see what you mean. I don't see why one of us didn't think of it long ago. Why, with wider tires, it wouldn't be half the work, would it? Especially when the ground's soft in the early spring, or after a rain! I say, that's a corking brain wave, old scout!"

Wattles coughed modestly but looked quite pleased in his solemn manner. Mr. Connover returned to his seat on the end of the bench just then and further discussion of the brilliant scheme was postponed. "You don't happen to know where I can get hold of a couple of good hitters for the Wolcott series, do you?" he asked smilingly as he sat down. "I could do with a couple, Deane."

"They should be left-handers, too, shouldn't they?" Loring asked lightly.

"Bless us, yes! But almost any sort would do. Just so long as they could hit the ball at least once in three times up! I don't hesitate to tell you, Deane, that unless this bunch finds its batting eye next Saturday we're going to look pretty small."

"And they're doing so well otherwise," said Loring. "It does seem too bad that they aren't hitting better."

"Well, you never can tell what a team will do when it has to do it, and I'm hoping that some of those chaps will come across day after tomorrow. I've seen it happen often enough." He told of a case in point, but Loring didn't pay very close attention, for he was thinking of the coach's opening remark. When the brief instance had been brought to a convincing close Loring said:

"You asked if I knew where you could get two hitters, sir. I don't, but I do know—at least—" Then he paused, in doubt.

"Well, don't leave me in suspense," prompted the coach, smiling. "What did you start to say?"

"I'm wondering whether I ought to say it," answered the boy, frowning perplexedly. "You see, he's a particular friend of mine, sir, and it may be that I'm—that he isn't as good as I think he is. I wouldn't want you to suppose that I was just trying to put something over on you."

"Don't trouble. I'll look after myself, Deane. Who have you in mind? Can he hit? Why haven't I seen him?"

"Oh, you've seen him all right," said Loring. "That's what makes me think he can't be as good as he seems to me. It's Clif Bingham I'm talking about, sir."

"Bingham?" echoed Steve. "Why, yes, I've seen Bingham often enough. He never struck me as being an exceptional hitter. He's still on the scrub, isn't he?"

"Yes, sir. I don't know whether you'd call him an exceptional hitter or not, Mr. Connover, but he's really done pretty well lately, and he's a left-hand batter."

"Hm. An outfielder, eh?"

"Centerfielder, sir."

"You say he's been hitting? Any idea what average he's made with the scrub?"

"No, sir, not much. About two seventy-five, I'd say. Maybe better lately. It wouldn't do any harm to—to have a look at him, would it? I guess—" Loring laughed—"I guess I could say more for him if he wasn't a particular chum of mine!"

Mr. Connover smiled, but absently. "Bingham," he muttered. "I remember him. Played good football last fall, didn't he? An outfielder, eh? Held his position regularly, Deane?"

"Well, for several weeks, sir. He beat out a fellow named Burke."

"I see." Mr. Connover's gaze strayed to the second diamond. "Look here, Deane, I can't leave this job. I wish you'd go over there and see what Bingham does and let me know later. Tell me how he batted and fielded; give me the full dope on him. Do you mind doing a bit of scouting?"

"No, sir, I'll be glad to. I meant to go over, anyway."

"Good! Don't be too optimistic, though. I doubt if Bingham can be used this year. But bring me a report on him just the same. Thanks. By the way, Deane, this is rather like assistant manager stuff, eh?"

When Loring reached the second team diamond, the game was already in its second inning, and the visitors had just annexed their first tally. Clif, however, fifth on the batting list, had still to make his initial trip to the plate, and when, after the enemy had been retired without further scoring, the second began to swing bats, Loring was conscious of a nervous anxiety that evidently communicated itself to Wattles. Wattles was breathing heavily, and, although he maintained his correct attitude throughout the succeeding six innings, there were moments when excitement threatened to upset it. Wattles liked Clif very much, but even if he hadn't Loring's attachment for the boy would have been sufficient to assure Wattles' loyalty.

Clif's first trip to the plate ended in fiasco, for after he had refused a delivery that the umpire called a strike and had allowed two balls to go past him he bit at an in-curve and the sphere dribbled half-way to the pitcher's box and was sped quickly to first for the second out of the inning. Having retired from a useless effort to reach base ahead of the ball, he came across to where Loring sat, grinning ruefully. "Rotten, wasn't it?" he asked. "That curve fooled me all right! Got it half-way up my bat. He doesn't seem very hard, either. Bet you I smash one the next time! What do you say? Drinks at Burger's!"

"You're on," said Loring eagerly. "And, listen, Clif, don't forget the thought business! You know, the old will power. Now's the chance to use it, old chap."

"Gee, you seem awfully keen about this game! Got any money on it?" Clif laughed and then became puzzled by Loring's serious countenance. "What's up?" he asked, scowling. His gaze shot to Wattles' face. Wattles looked more solemn than ever!

"There's more than money up," replied Loring gravely. He wished that he might tell Clif just what was up, but he thought it might not be fair. Before Clif could ask the meaning of the cryptic statement he went on, smiling to prove that he hadn't meant a thing by it. "I want you fellows to win your last game, naturally," he said. "And I want you to fatten your batting and fielding record, you chump. This is the last chance you'll get this year, isn't it?"

"Sure is. All right, you watch me. I'll throw my thought on that pitcher the next time and make him give me what I want! And if he does, just watch it travel!"

"I hope it does, Clif! And I hope you'll hit every time you're up!"

"Thanks for your good wishes," answered the other carelessly as he sauntered off toward the outfield. "We'll strive not to disappoint you."

They didn't, and after Loring was back in his room Wattles set forth for Number 21 West Hall bearing a slip of paper. On it in Loring's neat writing was this mysterious inscription:

A.B. 4; R. 1; 1B. 2; S.B. 1; S.H. 1; P.O. 2; A. 2; E. 0.

Coach Connover must have been able to translate that code and to approve its meaning, for the next forenoon Bi Longwell knocked at Number 17 West Hall and, finding the room empty, tore a leaf from a pocket memorandum book, scrawled on it with his fountain pen and set it prominently against the base of the electric lamp on the study table. And there Clif found it a half-hour later. After having perused its brief message twice, the first time with utter incredulity, the second time with amazed delight, he laid it reverently down on the table, thrust both hands into the pockets of his capacious knickers and grinned expansively about the room. Then he said "*Gosh!*" very softly, almost reverently. "*What do you know?*"

Finally he picked up the slip of paper again and bore it to the window and, after viewing it back and front, read the words once more. "Bingham: Report to Coach Connover at 4. Longwell."

CHAPTER XVIII
WYNDHAM WINS

POSSIBLY THE SCHOOL JANITOR remained behind in Cotterville that Saturday, but certainly everyone else connected with Wolcott Academy made the journey to Freeburg. Oh, well, of course the Principal didn't come, and a few of the other members of the faculty may have been absent, but no one missed them. The invading horde arrived by train and by motor, flaunting brown banners bearing the white Old English W, brown armbands, brown megaphones and brown ties. It took possession of the town's few lunchrooms and overflowed from the Inn. It wandered about the streets and over the school grounds in bunches of two or more, slightly patronizing, high-spirited and extremely confident. And at two o'clock it filled the third base stand and ran over onto the turf where it occupied a few settees filched from the gymnasium or disposed itself on the ground. By that time eight pitchers had warmed up in spite of the well-known fact that Ogden, for Wyndham, and Osterman, for Wolcott, were to start the engagement. When, at a few minutes after two of a cloudy, somewhat muggy afternoon, the Dark Blue trotted into the field Jeff Ogden went to the mound and the other three Wyndham pitchers retired to the bench. Save that Risley was catching, the Wyndham team was the same aggregation that had been beaten a week before by Horner. One Clifton Bingham, recently recruited member of the squad, sat very comfortably in the shade of the first base stand and had nothing to do save look on and enjoy the game. In view of which it may seem strange that his countenance expressed nothing that looked like appreciation!

Considering that that contest was a pitcher's battle from beginning to end, and that just one run was scored, it would be futile for me to pretend that it was, as some games are, a breathless, nerve-wracking affair. Of course, if you are extremely partisan and somewhat emotional you can derive excitement from almost any contest in which your team takes part, and the audience today must have been both, for it shouted, sang, howled, waved flags, megaphones, hats and score sheets and acted decidedly concerned during nine innings. And since, as already hinted, the afternoon was one of those afternoons when just to turn around induces perspiration, some eight or nine hundred spectators were reduced to a breathless, wilted mass long before the last man was retired.

Because in a series of two-out-of-three the capture of the first game brings a distinct advantage to the victor, both teams wanted today's contest hard and went after it. Each started its best pitcher and strongest batting list. Both Ogden and Osterman were left-handers, but the similarity went little further. Jeff was a sizeable youth, but Osterman was all of six feet tall, big-boned, lanky, long-armed, awkward in everything save pitching. He was held to be Ogden's superior as a twirler, and his record showed it. He was a fast-ball artist first and foremost, but he owned a few good curves. Like most left-hand pitchers he could on occasion become exceedingly wild.

Wolcott's first batsman reached first when Van Dyke fumbled Tyson's peg across the diamond. The ball trickled toward the stand, and the runner made the mistake of trying to get to second. Van recovered in time to throw him out to Hurry. A hit to left field followed, and when Risley threw to second to head off a steal Tom let the ball get through him and the runner went on to third and Wolcott howled gleefully. The third batsman flied out to Hurry. Jeff Ogden landed the ball against the next man's shoulder and he went to first. When he started for second Risley threw to shortstop and Hurry made a wonderful return to the plate in time to cut off the runner from third. One hit, two errors, no runs.

For Wyndham, Pat Tyson hit between first and second and stole a minute later. Greene struck out and so did Hurry Leland. Returning the compliment, Osterman put the ball against Gus Risley's ribs, and he took his base. With two down and two on, the best Raiford could do was foul out to Van Dyke. One hit, no errors, no runs.

Again Wolcott's first batter hit safely, although Hurry made a gallant try. The runner went no further than first, however, for succeeding men were disposed of by left fielder, third baseman—Tyson ran far for that foul—and pitcher. That was Jeff's first strike-out. Wyndham went out in one-two-three order, Osterman fanning Tom and Van Dyke, and Talbott hitting straight into first baseman's hands.

Tom made a neat capture of a grounder in the third and assisted at the first out. Foul catches by Van Dyke and Risley retired the enemy side. For Wyndham Ogden struck out on three pitched balls and Tyson flied to left field. Greene got the first pass of the game and went to third when Captain Leland singled across that bag. Wyndham shouted imploringly for a score. Risley hit to shortstop and the latter cut off Greene at the plate.

Wolcott opened the fourth in a manner that caused the home team sup-porters extreme distress. The first batter, after Jeff had got into a hole, landed on a straight ball and drove it over Talbott's head for three bags. Had the runner been a bit faster that hit might have become a home-run, and, even as it was, many questioned the wisdom of the coacher on third when he held up the runner there. Ogden struck out the next ambitious youth, but the subsequent batsman drove a hot one to Van Dyke. Van made a neat stop and pegged to the plate, and Wolcott's hope was shattered. Risley blocked the runner cleverly. A minute later Gus again earned a cheer when he threw down to Tom and spoiled the steal. Wyndham expressed relief by prolonged cheering.

The Dark Blue was also due with a sensation in that inning, for after Raiford had gone out at first, first baseman to pitcher, Tom came across with an exact duplicate of the enemy's shot into left, landing much tuckered on third base. But—and the game was duplicating oddly—he, too, failed to score, since Talbott hit a fly to first baseman and Van Dyke's effort to center was an easy catch.

Ogden fielded to Van Dyke for the first Wolcott out in the fifth, the next batsman hit to left and later stole second cleverly, and the next fell victim to Jeff's curves. A hit would still have meant a tally, but a long fly to right field ended the suspense. It was in the last of the fifth that Wyndham broke through the Brown's defense at last, and it was Ogden who paved the way. Jeff wasn't a hitter—few pitchers are, of course—and Osterman had disposed of him with ridiculous ease before. But this time Jeff laid back and wouldn't be coaxed to swing at the wide ones, with the result that before anyone quite realized it Osterman had wasted three balls and had but one strike on Jeff. Jeff may not have had much hope of hitting the next offer, but it was straight and fast and he swung. The ball arched into left field and put Jeff on second, quite a bit surprised, probably! Pat Tyson landed on the first offering and slammed it at Osterman who knocked it down and fielded it to first for the out. But Ogden was by that time safe on third, and Wyndham was making Rome howl. The coachers behind first and third shouted and cavorted, the crowd on each side of the diamond yelled and the Wolcott players babbled. And, apparently, the temperature shot up from around eight-four to somewhere around a hundred-and-four!

A sacrifice fly would go a long way toward winning that game, and doubtless the thought occurred to Coach Connover. Al Greene was the next man on the Wyndham list, and Al had not yet touched the ball with his bat, even to make a foul. The best he had done was to draw a pass on the occasion of his last appearance. So right there Greene's connection with the team was temporarily severed, and a rather nervous youth selected a bat, listened to

Steve's instructions and stepped to the plate. The umpire waved his mask in a request for silence and announced:

"For Wyndham, Bingham batting in place of Greene!"

I've stated that Clif was nervous, and so he was, but he tried very hard not to let the enemy battery surmise the fact, and he succeeded. First of all, after carefully annexing a sufficient amount of loam to his hands, he bid for the catcher's respect by moving his bat behind him in a way to suggest that the catcher had best move back a couple of inches. The catcher accepted the suggestion and wondered what this unknown would like to have served to him. Having no dope on anyone named Bingham, he had to stop wondering and call for a couple of inquiries. The first inquiry was an in-curve, and Clif looked it over attentively and retired a foot from the plate to let it by. The next was a high ball on the outside, and Clif let that alone, too, the umpire indorsing his judgment. Then Osterman let go with a fast one, knee high, and the count was two and one. The next was much the same and had little on it except a slight drop. Clif liked it and swung his bat against it and sped to first. Out in center field a youth with brown sleeves ran in a few yards, pulled the ball to him, set himself quickly and pegged to second baseman. And second baseman threw desperately home. But no one save a one-legged man with inflammatory rheumatism could have failed to score on that play, and Jeff, while his arm might be slightly weary by now, had full use of his legs. Long before the ball had settled into center fielder's hands the Wyndham rooters were on their feet—or their neighbors'—hailing the tally! Jeff romped across the plate yards ahead of the ball and somewhat more than half the audience went stark, staring mad!

Then Captain Leland did just what Clif had done, sending a long fly to center fielder, and the fifth, the wonderful fifth inning was over. And Wyndham was one beautiful big run to the good!

Well, so far as scoring was concerned that ended the game, for although there were anxious moments during the succeeding four innings, never again did either contestant get a man as far as third base. Both Ogden and Osterman tightened up and pitched headier ball than they had been pitching, and both infields played better. Wyndham got three more scattered hits and Wolcott four—including a scratch—but not one led to a tally. Neither Tom nor Clif hit again. Tom twice lifted flies to the outfield, and Clif, up but once more, in the seventh, was an easy out, pitcher to first base. It was in the first of the seventh that Wolcott made her biggest threat. Then her first man hit past Tyson for one and took second on a sacrifice out. Tom's fast handling of a liner killed him at third. Tom also had the honor of bringing the game to a joyful close when he ran well into the outfield and caught a Texas Leaguer.

Loring's score book showed, when it was all over and the tumult and the shouting had died, that Wyndham had made seven hits to Wolcott's eight and three errors to the opponent's two. But it also showed that she had won the game. A comparison of the rival pitchers showed that Osterman had struck out five men to Ogden's four, had issued two passes to Ogden's one and, like the latter, had hit one batsman. At the bat, however, Jeff had had far the best of the encounter, since, while Osterman had made no hits at all, Jeff had slammed out a two-bagger and subsequently scored the only run.

All this was discussed and rediscussed that evening wherever two or more delighted Wyndham fellows came together. And with it was discussed also the outlook for the next contest. For instance, Loring is holding forth to an audience composed of Tom, Clif and Mr. Cooper: "Tuesday's game will be a lot different. In the first place both teams will have to put in pitchers not so good as today's. I guess Mr. Connover will start with Moore. Moore's a left-hander, too, and he will probably argue that if Wolcott couldn't hit a left-hander today she won't be able to do much better Tuesday. Still, he might start Erlingby. In any case, our pitcher's going to be hit a heap harder than he was today, for those fellows are batters! And we'll be hitting more, too, probably, for whoever Wolcott puts in against us will be easier pickings than Osterman. We didn't do badly today, I'll say, for Osterman's a mighty good twirler. Anyhow, Tuesday's game will be a batting fest, and the side which bats the hardest will win. We will be on the other fellow's field, too, and that's against us somewhat. I don't know how Tuesday's game is going to come out, but I do know that it's going to be a harder game to score than today's was! You're going, aren't you, Mr. Cooper?"

Mr. Cooper nodded, and the many little wrinkles about his eyes danced. "Try to keep me away," he answered.

CHAPTER XIX
WALKING PAPERS

THE TRIUMVIRATE WERE SEATED under the maples on the lawn. It was Sunday afternoon, and the hot weather continued, although there was rather more life in the air than there had been yesterday. Clif and Tom had discarded coats, an example set them by numerous other youths who dotted the shaded expanse beyond East Hall. Mr. Cooper, strolling over from the Inn, found them there and joined the small circle. Loring and Clif were attempting to arrange a meeting in France or Switzerland in the summer, and Mr. Cooper, having seated himself on the grass, leisurely filled his pipe and listened, with only an occasional word of comment. Loring's family would be abroad all summer, while Clif and his father had only some six weeks to spend on the other side; facts which made it difficult for the two boys to agree on a place and time of meeting. Tom had nothing to say until, presently, Mr. Cooper remarked: "I fancy you'd like a bit of that, Tom."

Tom shrugged. "Oh, no, I'd hate it! I couldn't be happy outside the dear old State of New Jersey."

"You're out of it now," said Clif.

"And no better off," answered Tom. "New Jersey—Connecticut—what's the diff?"

"I wish you could be over there, too," said Loring with evident sincerity. "Say, wouldn't we have a corking time, the three of us?"

"The Triumvirate in the Alps," mused Clif. "Sounds like a story, doesn't it? Gee, I wish you could make it, too, Tom. No hope, I suppose? I mean you couldn't possibly persuade Mr. Whatshisname that he needs a vacation?"

"If I could he'd take it at Asbury Park," replied Tom disconsolately. "Heck, I don't believe he even knows there *is* such a place as Europe!"

"You might try the 'old will power,'" suggested Mr. Cooper. "After what it's done here, you know, eh?"

"I'd like to see anyone will that guardian of mine to do anything he didn't want to!" said Tom bitterly. "Anyway, I've about decided that that psychology stuff is the bunk. I don't believe it had anything to do with our making the first team, and I don't believe Clif thinks it did, either."

"Well, I do think so," declared Clif stoutly. "Why, look here, Tom, when I started out I had just about as much chance of making the nine as—as I have of finding my name down in the First Ten tomorrow! And then, all of a sudden, Steve grabs me! If it wasn't because we fellows kept thinking and willing, what was it because of?"

Tom laughed jeeringly. "Don't credit me with any of it, Clif, for I haven't done a nickel's worth of willing for more than a week. I just haven't had time to think about it. Sorry, old chap, but you might as well have the truth. I've been too busy to put my mind on your affairs. Now let's hear from Loring."

"I'm going to disappoint you," said Loring. "I haven't quit, Tom. The old will power's still working sixteen hours a day. One for all, you know, and all for one!"

"Well, I sort of forgot," muttered Tom. "You fellows must have done it single—no, double-handed."

"It's sort of funny about that," confessed Clif. "Fact is, I don't believe I've done much—much concentrating myself lately. That is, not consciously. I suppose what happened was that I'd got sort of in the habit of doing it and—and just did it without realizing."

Tom sniffed skeptically, but Loring said gravely, "That must be it, Clif." He had not told Clif of that talk with the coach and the subsequent "scouting," nor did he tell him about it until many weeks later. Mr. Cooper broke in on the momentary silence.

"If I were you, Tom," he said, "I'd keep it up. The will power stuff, I mean; concentration and all that, eh? No harm in trying, you know. Wouldn't be a bit surprised to run across the whole lot of you over there later on."

"Well, *I'd* be surprised if you did, mightily surprised!" retorted Tom. "Unless 'over there' means Asbury Park!"

"Oh, no," replied Mr. Cooper seriously, "Switzerland. You never can tell."

Tom looked at him incredulously, opened his lips to speak, thought better of it and subsided.

"Gosh," sighed Clif, "it's hard to realize that we'll be all through here Wednesday! That I'll be having lunch at home the next day! And taking in a ball game in the afternoon, maybe, and going to a movie in the evening!"

"I suppose you've got through finals all right, Loring," said Tom. "It must be funny not to have to worry any about them."

"Yes, I'm fairly certain of passing," replied Loring. "How about you?"

"Me? Oh, I'll get by," answered Tom doggedly. "Somehow. I can't just figure it out, but I have a hunch that I'll make it. Got to if I want to come back next year."

Tom's hunch proved correct, thanks to a fortunate and, to him, quite inexplicable *B* in Hygiene. Loring's name was on the list in the First Ten of the third class, and Clif barely failed of winning that distinction. Although Tom had professed his certainty of passing, the news that he had scraped through appeared to bring him a vast relief and a noticeable elevation of spirits. He felt so good all the forenoon that it required earnest efforts on the part of Clif and Billy Desmond to keep him from breaking a window as a testimonial of joy. Dissuaded from this course, he set out for the Inn to announce the glad tidings to Mr. Cooper. The latter seemed quite as pleased as Tom.

"Of course," Tom acknowledged, "I haven't got much to boast of. If 'Cocky' hadn't given me that *B* in Hygiene I'd have failed. The only thing I'm afraid of is that he made a mistake and will find it out before Wednesday! Alick was pretty good to me, too; better than I thought he would be. I've been a good deal of a trial to him all year, and he might have socked me an awful wallop if he'd wanted to. He's a pretty square old guy, Alick! I guess Mr. Winslow will cut up a bit when he sees my marks, but he can't say I didn't pass." Tom was frowningly thoughtful a moment. "Something tells me he's going to be disappointed. I have an idea he'd be glad of an excuse to take me away from here. He's always reminding me of how much it costs. Well, I fooled him this time!"

"Can't you stay and have lunch with me?" asked Mr. Cooper a few minutes later.

"Thanks, but I can't, sir. You see, I'm at training table now, and Steve makes us all toe the mark. Sorry, sir. I'd like to."

Practice was called for two-thirty, since there were no more classes, and, having nothing particular to do after dinner, Tom went over to the gymnasium at a few minutes before two. He had lost track of Clif and expected to find him in the locker room. Whether Clif was there Tom didn't discover, for, he didn't reach the locker room until very much later. Fate ordained that he should encounter Coles just short of the entrance, and in ordaining that Fate played a scurvy trick on Tom.

Ever since he had been deposed from second base by Tom, Wink Coles had nursed a grievance. He hadn't shown the fact to any extent, and the friendly relations between the two had not been noticeably affected. They had never been very close, even in the fall, when both had played on the Fighting Scrub, as last season's second eleven had been dubbed. Wink had fully expected to play second base throughout the spring, and he had been sadly disappointed when Tom had been elevated from the scrub nine and he, Wink, had been relegated to the position of an infield substitute. Only a few hours before the encounter with Tom he had learned that in two studies in which he had fully expected *B*'s he had been awarded *C*'s. He had passed, but he had done it by a margin not very much wider than Tom's, and he was still disgruntled. In short, Wink Coles was in a state of mind hardly to be classed as genial, and it was unfortunate that Tom, still in an expansive mood, should have chosen that particular opportunity to be affable.

"Hello, Wink!" he greeted, refusing to be satisfied with the nod and grunt they usually exchanged on meeting. "How'd you come out?"

"All right," replied Wink gloomily, continuing to lean against the wall and stare into the sunlit distance. "How'd you?"

It was plainly to be understood that he didn't care a continental about Tom's fate, but Tom was not critical of tones. He answered smilingly and flippantly.

"Great! In the First Ten—counting from the bottom! I'm still wondering how it happened."

"You're a lucky dub, anyhow," replied Wink unflatteringly.

"I was lucky this time," agreed Tom, with what may have seemed to the other a distinctly irritating laugh. That would have ended the conversation if Tom hadn't remembered that he had lots of time on his hands. He didn't particularly care for Wink, but he wanted to talk to someone and, failing another, Wink would answer. "They say it's better to be born lucky than rich," Tom went on.

"I guess it is," said Wink. "And I'll say you're sure lucky!" At last it dawned on Tom that the other was not in absolute sympathy. In fact, Wink's tone of voice had been a trifle—well, a trifle mean! Tom became inquiring in look and speech.

"Sounds like a nasty crack, Wink," he said less genially. "What's on your mind?"

"Well," answered Wink, eying him coldly, "I guess you were pretty lucky to land on the nine, weren't you?"

"Oh! That's what's eating you, eh? Yes, I guess there was some luck in that, but I wouldn't say it was all luck. Sorry I crowded you, Wink, but I couldn't help it, you know. Fortunes of war, and all that, eh?"

"Oh, sure!" replied Wink sarcastically. "Fortunes of war and a lot of luck, Kemble."

Tom frowned. "Heck, what are you so sore about? You didn't own that position, did you? Anyway, why don't you tell your stuff to Steve? What's the idea of blaming it all on me?"

"Who said I was blaming you?" asked Wink. "And I guess you're right, at that. Luck's pretty good, but standing in with the coach is a blame sight better, I guess."

"Is that *so*?" inquired Tom. "Meaning I swiped for that job, eh? You've got a crust!"

"Oh, I'm not saying you swiped." Wink laughed annoyingly. "You didn't have to, I guess. Steve has his friends, and ever since last fall you've been one of them. Lots of fellows thought it was mighty funny when he jumped you from the scrub, Kemble."

Tom smiled. If Wink had known him a good deal better he would have recognized that particular kind of a smile as a danger signal. "Coles," said Tom gently, "those cracks about me don't bother me a mite, but when you say that Steve Connover isn't straight you've started something. Listen to this, and get it. You're a dirty pup."

Wink struck swiftly, but Tom was ready. He stepped back quickly and held up a hand. "Cut it out!" he said. "I'm not going to be fired on account of you. I'll fight you all right, but we'll fight regularly tomorrow morning."

"You'll fight now!" gasped Wink. "You called me a pup, you—you rotten swiper!" He struck again and landed glancingly on Tom's neck. Tom backed away, shooting a hasty glance about. Fortunately, although there were a score or more of fellows over on the scrub diamond, no one was apparently looking toward the gymnasium steps. Wink was following, eloquent on the subject of Tom's character. Tom shrugged.

"All right," he said grimly. "I'll fight now, but not here. Come around the corner."

"You bet you'll fight!" raged Wink Coles, following the other. "You'll fight or I'll chase you all over the lot!"

"Save your breath," advised Tom, and went down the steps, slipping out of his coat as he went.

Five minutes later a scandalized first classman hurried over from the tennis courts, followed by a squad of interested schoolmates, and hurled the combatants apart. Even Wink realized authority when he met it, and if he hadn't there were enough assistant peace-makers to quell him. The first classman delivered a scorching oration, declared that it was his duty to report the offenders at once, made it plain that he had no intention of doing any such thing and finally calmed down enough to offer advice.

"You fellows cut in there before anyone else sees you and get Dan to fix you up. You're disgusting, both of you! You ought to know better than pull this stuff. Shut up!" This to Wink, attempting a defense through one side—the unbattered side—of his mouth. "I don't want to hear anything about it! Get in there, I tell you. And if you want my advice I'll tell you you'd better keep away from the faculty the rest of the day!"

Some fifteen minutes later Mr. Connover stopped in front of Wink Coles and gazed at him in surprise. Wink looked extremely disreputable. Steve hesitated, walked on, turned back and spoke. "Who did that to you, Coles?" he asked. Wink looked away, encountered the amused faces of his mates and muttered unintelligibly. Steve frowned. As a member of the faculty it was his duty to report for discipline any infraction of the rules, and there was a stern injunction against fighting save at a certain place and under established regulations. The regulations provided that an affair of honor must be laid before a member of the upper class whose duty it was to inquire thoroughly into the merits of the matter and, if in his judgment a meeting was advisable, appoint a referee and set the time of the combat. Then, each principal having selected a second, the affair was pulled off with as little publicity as possible and under prize-ring rules behind the stable. These meetings were held in the early morning, and Mr. Connover had only to view Wink's countenance to know that its unlovely appearance was of short standing. Still, members of the faculty were permitted discretion, and sometimes it was considered unwise to pursue researches too far. Mr. Connover viewed the embarrassed Wink a moment longer, as though lending full consideration to that muttered explanation, and then said briefly: "You're excused for the day, Coles."

And that was that. And just when the incident was losing savor for the players, and Dan, the trainer, was emptying the baseballs out on the turf, a new sensation arrived in the person of Tom. If Wink was disreputable, Tom was unfit for publication! And he knew it. Hurrying so as not to be late, he yet tried very hard to reach his goal without notice, and with the latter desire uppermost in his mind, he skirted the first base stand and attempted to slip into the throng as modestly as possible. But when you have two areas of plaster decorating your face and a strip of the same glaring material across the knuckles of one hand your chance of attaining obscurity is slim. There arose a delighted if restrained cheer from his teammates as Tom, affecting nonchalance, stepped into the shadow of Cobham and tried the experiment of fitting a left-hand glove over a painful right. Having recognized the futility of that attempt, Tom picked up a trickling ball, turned his back toward the coach and wandered down the line. Surreptitious remarks greeted him, but Tom appeared too intent on duty for mere persiflage. He didn't really have much hope of escaping the vigilant eye of Mr. Connover, but at least he could postpone the evil moment he thought. If only the coach would send the first team into the field—

"Kemble!"

Tom stopped as though shot, hesitated and turned innocently toward the speaker. The coach had trailed him along the base line, almost to first, and he looked very angry. Tom's heart sank, but he attempted a blithe smile, which hurt him considerably, and responded: "Yeth, thir?"

"So you've been fighting again, have you?" demanded Steve in a voice that reminded Tom of a blue chisel. "Getting to be rather a habit with you, isn't it?"

"Yeth—*no*, thir!" Tom wished he didn't have to lisp like that. It sounded so silly! But the inside of his mouth was very sore, and his cheek and his tongue and his lower lip got in each other's way horribly. He was well aware that he presented a lamentable, even a humorous appearance, and he looked hopefully at the coach, thinking that either sympathy or amusement would break the glacial set of the latter's features. But Mr. Connover had been presented with one too many incapacitated players this afternoon, and neither pity nor amusement swayed him.

"I've sent Coles off for the day," said the coach, "and you may go, too. Only you needn't come back, Kemble. I shan't need you any more this season."

Tom was stunned. There was one awful instant of silence and then he broke into protests. "Honeth, Mither Connover, 'twath'nt my fault! I—I didn't mean—"

"You got into a fight at Greenville," said the coach coldly. "I let that go. But this time I'm through. I'm forced to the conclusion that you're simply a trouble-maker, Kemble. I don't want your sort on the nine. I ought to report you at the Office. That is my duty as a faculty member. But I'm going to deal with you merely as a coach. Possibly the loss of your place on the team will be enough to show you—"

"I with you'd let me tell you, pleathe, thir! Honeth, I didn't thtart it, thir. You thee—"

"That will do, Kemble. I don't want your excuses. You've been fighting with Coles, contrary to school regulations, and I'm letting you off pretty easy with the loss of your place on the squad. There's no more to be said. I want you to leave the field this instant."

"Yeth, thir." Tom attained a certain dignity then, not an easy thing to do under the circumstances. "I'm thorry, Mither Connover."

"So am I, Kemble." The tone was not quite so hard, but Tom didn't make the mistake of thinking that it presaged relenting. "Mither Connover" turned away and strode back to his duties, and Tom, trying hard to keep his eyes clear of tears, went straight for the gymnasium. Before he had reached it self-pity gave way to anger against Coles. He would, he concluded, get his togs off and go in search of Wink. And when he found him he would start where he had left off and finish the job! No, sir, it didn't make a bit of difference to him whether he got fired or not now. If he couldn't play any more baseball what use was there sticking around the rotten hole? Something had told him long ago that he wasn't going to like Wyndham, and now he hated it!

He wondered where Wink Coles could be found. Probably in his room. Tom managed a crooked smile at the thought of how that room would look when he was through with Wink. Then the smile faded before a look of exasperation, for he couldn't for the life of him remember where Wink roomed! Well, he could find out. Loring had a catalogue. He had seen it on the lower shelf of the bookcase only last evening. And Loring would be out, for Tom had glimpsed him at the far end of the bench when he had slipped past the end of the stand. Yes, and Mr. Cooper had been there, too; sitting back of third base; seeing the whole rotten business. That was tough! He wished Mr. Cooper hadn't witnessed his degradation. Mr. Cooper was—well, Tom thought a good deal of Mr. Cooper and valued his respect. And that reminded him that Mr. Cooper had wanted so much to have him pass, and had shown such pleasure just that morning when he had heard the news. And now, Tom reflected uneasily, he was going to get himself fired out of school, and Mr. Cooper would be horribly disappointed in him. Somehow the idea of beating up Wink Coles some more lost its appeal. Besides, come to think of it, Wink had done a lot more beating up than he had! Wink was a year older and about twelve pounds heavier and no dumbbell when it came to the wallops! Tom acknowledged a grudging respect for Wink. Still, that didn't cut any ice. Even if he got licked good and plenty, he would manage to make Wink look a lot worse than he did now before he was through! Only there was Mr. Cooper, and Mr. Cooper was a corking chap, and—

And just then Tom reached the silent locker room, and there was Wink, sitting on a bench, his legs sprawled before him and his gaze fixed disconsolately on space. But he looked around when Tom clumped in on his spikes, and the two stared at each other for a brief moment without speech. Then each averted his gaze and Tom pulled open the door of his locker and began to unlace a shoe. Silence was heavy. Tom wondered why he didn't go across and challenge the foe to a renewal of hostilities. They'd probably have the place to themselves long enough to reach a decision. It wasn't that he was afraid—although, to be quite frank, the passing thought of having to hit anything with his bruised hand again was distinctly unpleasant—but the savor seemed to have gone out of the project. Tom kicked the first shoe off and started on the other. Then Wink's voice sounded hollowly in the room.

"Think he will let us back tomorrow?" asked Wink.

"You," growled Tom. "Not me. I'm fired. For keeps."

There was a long moment of silence. Then:

"How does he get that way?" demanded Wink indignantly. "He didn't tell me I was fired. He just said I was excused for today. How come he socks you like that?"

Tom gave up trying to undo an obdurate knot and faced his recent antagonist. "Says I'm a trouble-maker. I had a bit of a rumpus with a guy over in Greenville the day we played there, and Steve got onto it and was mighty decent. Then, today—oh, I suppose he couldn't help thinking I was a rough-neck. Said fighting was a habit with me and he didn't want any of my kind on the team."

Another silence broken finally with: "That's not fair, Tom. It was my fault. You didn't want to fight me then. I made you."

"Oh, well." Tom shrugged. "I didn't have to, I guess."

"Sure, you had to! Say, you needn't believe it if you don't want to, but I'm mighty sorry. Tell you what I'll do—"

"You'll do nothing," replied Tom emphatically. "One of us is enough. Oh, heck, I guess I deserve what I got. It was a fool stunt!"

"Sure was," agreed Wink sadly.

"Well, what in time did you go and start it for?" demanded Tom with pardonable asperity. "I don't see yet what you had to get so blamed nasty about!"

"I know," acknowledged Wink humbly. "It was pretty rotten. I was sore, that's all. About losing my place on the team, and not getting better marks after I'd worked like the dickens all spring; and you being so thundering pleased with yourself and—and everything! I sort of went flooey. I'm awfully sorry, Tom. Honest!"

"All right," answered the other hurriedly. "Guess I know how you felt. Just rotten luck, that's all. Forget it, Wink."

"I wish you'd let me tell Steve just what happened; how it started and all."

"Swell scheme!" jeered Tom. "Tell him you said he was playing favorites, eh? You'd make a hit with him!"

"I wouldn't care," muttered Wink. "Besides, I was only talking. I know Steve's square just as well as you do."

"You do!" Tom stared in amazement. "Well, I'll be switched! Then why—what—"

Wink shrugged disconsolately. "I just wanted to make you mad, I suppose."

"Huh! Well, you did it! But you keep away from Steve!"

CHAPTER XX
CLIF GETS AN ERROR

THE GATHERING OF THE Triumvirate in Loring's room that Monday evening was rather gloomy for awhile. Tom's news affected them all. Loring was so disturbed by it that presently Tom was forced to assume a cheerfulness he was far from feeling in order to rescue the other from the dumps. "Oh, well," said Tom, grinning heroically, "I did better than I expected to, anyway. When I started out in February I didn't really have any hope of making the first team, but I did make it and I played in several games, and so it isn't so bad, eh?"

"Where you made your big mistake," said Clif, "was in going over to the field after that scrap. Why didn't you send word that you were sick or something and ask for a cut?"

"Yes, I guess I pulled a boner there, Clif. But you know how Steve is about missing practice. He'd have been around to see me this evening, probably, and I'd have been just as bad off. You see," concluded Tom ingenuously, "I thought maybe he wouldn't notice anything."

That naïve statement brought the first laugh of the evening. The idea of anyone short of a blind man failing to notice Tom's plastered and discolored face was certainly amusing! Mr. Cooper, rather to Tom's relief, seemed less inclined to blame the latter for that set-to with Coles than did the others. Of course neither Clif nor Loring bore down heavily on that phase of the disaster, but Tom knew very well that they considered him culpable. Mr. Cooper seemed to be more interested in the fact that Tom had fought in defense of Mr. Connover than in the fact that he had transgressed school regulations. He even suggested tentatively that possibly Mr. Connover, could the whole story be laid before him, might be moved to leniency. But Tom rejected the idea. "That would be just like swiping," he said. "Wink wanted to go and tell Steve that stuff, but I said he shouldn't. Besides, I'm not so certain I fought Wink because he dragged Steve in. Maybe it was just because he got me good and mad."

Mr. Cooper refused that theory with a shake of his head, but Clif, not yet won to sympathy, muttered: "You're always going off half-cocked, you crazy coot!"

Presently the talk turned to the morrow's game once more, and Tom discovered that, even though he must witness it from the stand instead of the diamond, he could find interest in speculation and discussion. Loring, Mr. Cooper and Wattles were to make the trip to Cotterville, which was some twenty-six miles distant, in a hired automobile, and now it was arranged that Tom should make a fourth in the party. Clif would, of course, go with the players in one of the motor buses. Whether he would start the game in the outfield was another subject for speculation. Clif thought it would depend on whether Wolcott used a left-hand or right-hand pitcher.

"He had Greene playing center most of the time today," he said, "and that looks as if Al was the favorite. Say, Tom, you and Coles certainly put Steve on his ear today. He was sure grouchy!"

"I don't see that you can blame him," observed Loring. "Saturday he had a nice infield that worked together like the insides of a clock. Now he's got to put Coles in at second base, and he hasn't played there regularly for weeks! Why shouldn't he get peeved? It's enough to make any coach mad!"

"I guess that's right," sighed Clif. "I guess he has a hunch that we're going to get smeared tomorrow."

"Heck, why should we?" demanded Tom. "Didn't we beat them Saturday? Why can't we do it again?"

"For several reasons," answered Clif tartly. "One of 'em is that you've spilled the beans, you poor fish!"

"Aw, shut up," growled Tom unhappily.

There had been talk of Cobham behind the plate for Wyndham in Tuesday's game, but evidently Cob wasn't quite ready for duty again since it was Gus Risley who donned the mask when the last half of the first inning began that afternoon at Cotterville. But Gus had done a good job before, and if Wyndham was to meet with defeat it probably wouldn't be due to the catcher. The Dark Blue had sent but three men to bat in the first of the inning and Rice, the Wolcott left-hander, had disposed of them easily. Sam Erlingby was in the points for Wyndham. Sam was a right-hander, but as Wolcott had touched up Ogden, who pitched from the port side, pretty frequently on Saturday it was thought that Sam would prove as effective as either of Wyndham's remaining possibilities, Moore and Frost. Sam started off badly with a pass, but after that he settled down and soon had the side out.

Clif was in center field, rather to his surprise, and, although he didn't know it yet, was in for a busy afternoon. His first chance came in the second when, after Talbott had been retired, pitcher to first base, for Wyndham's third out, the Wolcott shortstop, first up, lifted a fly to the outfield. Both Clif and Raiford made for it, for the ball was hit to short field and might have been ticketed for either of them. Clif, however, had started quicker than the right fielder, and Captain Leland's cry of "Bingham! Bingham!" caused Raiford to slacken. Clif hardly dared hope to make that catch, but he did, picking it at last with his knuckles almost scraping the turf. Of course, he went headlong, but he held tightly to the ball and scrambled back to his feet to the sound of wild cheering from the Wyndham side of the field. Wyndham had come to Cotterville with the fine determination to grab off this contest and settle the series here and now. Not more than a handful of fellows had remained behind, the cheer leaders were on their feet constantly and the Dark Blue's rooters were enthusiastically responsive to demands. They seemed to have made up their minds that if the victory depended on noise it was to be theirs!

There was no scoring until the fifth. Then, after Clif had just failed to beat the ball to first—he had struck out abjectly his first time up—and Talbott had popped a weak fly to third baseman, Van Dyke whacked a hard one over first base and got to second by a hair's breadth. Sam Erlingby got into the hole and then waited for the pitcher to even the score. Then he swung mightily at what was meant for a third strike, and the ball glanced off his bat and went bounding toward third base. Third baseman came in hard, sought to scoop the ball up one-handed, missed it and both runners were safe. It remained for Pat Tyson to produce a score, and Pat came across with a clean hit into left that sent Van Dyke scampering across the plate with the initial tally of the game. But that ended the scoring for another inning, for Erlingby was out at third when Raiford hit to shortstop, and Wolcott, although she got a runner to second, was not yet able to solve Erlingby's slants.

Wyndham went down expeditiously in the sixth and the audience began to wonder if this was to be another 1 to 0 game. Wolcott answered the question speedily, however, for the sixth was the Brown's big inning. Rice, the pitcher, started the trouble with a short fly that Wink Coles was unable to capture, although he made a gallant attempt. A sacrifice put Rice on second. Then Erlingby let down and, presto, the three bags were occupied, there was but one man away and the Wolcott shortstop, a hard hitter, was up. Erlingby pitched two balls without getting a strike across, and then a halt was called and Sam retired, cheered by his schoolmates but looking rather dejected. Coach Connover selected Bud Moore to carry on the game. To some it seemed that Jeff Ogden might have been his choice, but since Jeff would be called on to pitch tomorrow it was doubtless the part of wisdom to give him the benefit of another day's rest. Bud faced a hard task and began it none too well when the best he could do was put one strike over and then pitch two more balls, forcing in the tying run.

A liner to Coles was knocked down, but he messed up the recovery of the ball and the runner from third was safe at the plate by inches only. However, Risley's quick throw to third got the next runner for the second out. A long fly to left field was misjudged by Talbott, and a third tally came in. Another fly, this time to center field, sent Clif speeding back and back until it seemed to him that he must presently crash into the wall of the dormitory there. But he didn't get quite to the building, and when the ball came down he was luckily under it, and the big inning came to an end right then.

But three to one looked bad when the seventh inning began, and no better when the first half of it was over. Hurry got a hit, but Risley, Coles and Clif went out miserably. Wolcott took to the foe's new twirler enthusiastically in the last of the inning but hit safely only once. Clif had two easy flies for the second and third outs. Wyndham shouted hoarsely, imploringly, for runs when the eighth started, and Pat Tyson, head of the Dark Blue's batting list, stepped to the plate. But the best Pat could do was a foul to first baseman. Raiford, however, brought joy and hope with a long single to right field, and Captain Leland's bunt along first base line, after being allowed plenty of time to roll foul, decided to remain fair, and there were two on. Wyndham went quite crazy with delight and blue pennants waved mightily.

Gus Risley was not a certain hitter, but he was capable of sending a ball far when he connected with it. On the present occasion, though, Gus was much too eager to hit, and in the end a fly to right field sent him back to the bench and the runners to second and third. Wink Coles was derricked in favor of a pinch hitter, Sim Jackson. Sim was canny and waited while Rice delivered a ball, a strike and a second ball. Then he tried at one and missed it. Rice sent a third ball over and then, while Sim watched operations narrowly, pitched into the dirt for the fourth ball. Wyndham again rose to unprecedented heights of sound! Three on, two down! Clif, whose turn it was, looked questionably at Mr. Connover. It seemed to Clif that right here was an excellent spot into which to insert another pinch hitter. But the coach only nodded and didn't even give him instructions, and Clif went out to the plate feeling horribly anxious and impotent. But the Wolcott pitcher helped vastly to restore his equanimity by sending over something so wide of the rubber that only a marvellous acrobatic stunt by the catcher prevented a wild pitch. After that, amidst the delighted booing of the visitors, Rice offered another ball, and the Wolcott coach signaled from the bench and the Brown changed pitchers.

Dobbel, the succeeding artist, was a right-hander, and was said to have nothing very much except a good out-curve and a slow ball with a considerable break. He started out by fooling Clif on a curve and then tried the same thing again and heard the umpire call it a ball. He looked pained and pitched a straight one. At least, it looked straight until Clif swung at it. Clif missed it by inches, it seemed. The next one had to be good, and Clif kept his eyes glued fast on the pitcher and then on the oncoming sphere. Then he swung and hit and raced for first. Second baseman made a wild stab for the flying ball but missed it. Clif stopped at first. The ball came back from right fielder and was relayed home by the pitcher, but Raiford and Leland were safe and the score was tied! And then, before anyone quite knew what was happening, Sim was being run down between second and third! Clif, half-way to second, scuttled back, but he might as well have kept on, for Jackson finally dashed for third and was tagged.

Then came the last of the eighth, with Wyndham and Wolcott both shouting wildly and very, very hoarsely, with blue and brown pennants swirling and with Fortune still impartial. And in the last of the eighth the Wyndham infield, which had gone along well enough so far, cracked wide open!

Captain Leland made the first miscue when he took an easy bounder and snapped it across the diamond well over Van's head. The runner went on to second without having to slide. A minute later Pat Tyson fumbled and there were two on. Out in center field Clif watched miserably and chewed grass stalks as fast as he could pluck them. Then came a chance for a double, Leland to Coles to Van Dyke, and this time it was Wink who spilled the beans. He made the out at second but threw so far to the left of first that Van Dyke had to go off his bag for the ball. There were runners now on first and third with only one down. A well-timed steal put the second runner on the middle sack. Then the batter found something of Moore's that he liked the looks of and there was a mighty *crack*. On bases the brown-legged runners poised, ready for their sprints, while the ball arched far into center field. Clif turned and ran out to the left a few yards, judged the ball again and stepped back. It would be an easy catch, he knew, and yet the proceedings so far in that inning had given him a troubled mind, and now, as the ball came dropping slowly toward him, he became obsessed with a sudden foreboding of failure. He tried to thrust it away from him in the brief moment that remained, but it clung. Then his hands went up and the ball slapped into his glove and a great relief flooded him as he stepped forward for the throw and swung his hand back. And then the thing happened. For an instant he had held the ball securely, it had seemed, yet when he threw his arm backward it was no longer in his hand!

He saw it at his feet an instant later, seized it and, raging at himself, sped it to Coles. But the deed was done by the time Wink got the ball. Two more runs had been scored, there was a man on first and there was still but one out. Wyndham sat down again, comparatively silent for once, and pondered defeat. Out in center field a miserable youth stared fixedly at the diamond, unheeding Sid Talbott's "Hard luck, Clif!", calling himself all the uncomplimentary things his mind could think of and wishing very, very hard that he didn't have to walk in there presently and face that crowded stand.

Yet the actuality wasn't nearly so bad as the anticipation, for none of his teammates showed by word or look that he had failed them, while the audience, having witnessed a smart double play by Moore, Leland and Van Dyke, had for the time forgotten that fiasco of his. But Tom didn't forget it. He watched gloomily while Talbott fanned, Van Dyke bunted to third baseman and was thrown out and Bud Moore popped an easy fly to shortstop. Then he listened gloomily while the defeat was discussed from every angle in the dressing room. And finally he sat, moody and disconsolate, in the bus and rattled and swayed back to Freeburg. He found no relief from the knowledge of defeat, as did the others, in talking largely of what would happen tomorrow. In fact, he was pretty certain that he would have no share in the morrow's happenings!

CHAPTER XXI
WATTLES INTERVENES

RETURNING FROM COTTERVILLE, TOM alone of the four occupants of the car was downcast. Loring had discounted the defeat, Mr. Cooper accepted it with cheerful philosophy and Wattles maintained a thoughtful silence that, unnoted by the others, was at moments slightly perturbed, even anxious. He listened to the discussion, which lasted most of the way to Freeburg, but volunteered speech only once. Then he inquired of Loring: "If Mr. Tom had taken part, sir, we might have won, do you think?"

Loring said "Yes," and Tom grunted. "I might have been worse than any of them," he said. "You can't tell. One fellow slips up and then the whole infield goes on the blink. It's catching!"

"Just the same," replied Loring, "I wish you were going to be in there tomorrow!"

After the school had been reached, Wattles attended to Loring's comfort and then with a cough said: "If you'll not be needing me for a short time, sir, there's a small matter I'd like to attend to."

Loring, studying the score he had kept of the afternoon's game, nodded absently. "I'm all right. Don't hurry back, Wattles."

"Thank you, sir." Wattles set his black derby very carefully in place and departed.

Mr. Connover lived in Number 21 West Hall, and thither Wattles made his way. His knock on the door brought a faint invitation to enter, and when he had done so a voice proceeding from the bathroom called, "Make yourself at home. I'll be out in a minute." Wattles sat down in a chair, placed his derby crosswise on his knees and placed a hand on each end of the brim, quite as though he feared a strong gust of wind might whisk the precious hat away. The minute became several minutes, and then the baseball coach emerged from the bedroom, tying the cords of his bath-robe and looking very clean and cheerful.

"Ah, it's Wattles," he said.

"Yes, sir." Wattles arose to make the admission.

"Well, sit down. What can I do for you? Or, I suppose, Mr. Deane."

"I took the liberty of coming on my own account, sir," replied Wattles a trifle nervously.

"Oh! Well, glad to see you. Just what—ah—"

"Mr. Connover, I witnessed the game this afternoon, and I saw how things are going. Our infield, sir, is not—" Wattles hesitated and shook his head gently—"is not what it should be."

Steve looked distinctly surprised. "I didn't know you were a fan, Wattles. However, what you say is absolutely true. Our infield leaves much to be desired. Or it did this afternoon."

"Yes, sir, and that's why I took the liberty of coming. I'd like to speak to you about Mr. Tom, sir."

"Who's Mr. Tom, Wattles?"

"Mr. Kemble, sir, I should say."

"Oh, I see. Well, frankly, Wattles, I wouldn't bother. That incident is closed. I don't think there is anything you could say that would help Kemble to get his position back, and that, I imagine, is what you are here for. I appreciate your interest, Wattles, but really it's no good."

"Very well, sir. Then may I tell you what I learned about the young gentleman simply as a—simply as a matter of interest? That is, sir, if I'm not taking your time from more important affairs."

"That part's all right. I've nothing to do until supper time, but— Oh, all right, Wattles, shoot!"

So Wattles shot. He made rather a long story of it, choosing his words very carefully as was proper when conversing with a member of the faculty. And when he had finally finished Mr. Connover asked: "Wattles, are you quite sure you've got that right?"

"Oh, absolutely, sir. I was in Mr. Loring's room when Mr. Tom told about it. The facts are just as I've stated them, sir."

"Hm." Mr. Connover shook his head in smiling exasperation. "It would have been a lot simpler if you hadn't told me this, Wattles. Of course, I didn't know that Kemble had taken up arms on my account, and I'll not deny that it makes a difference in my personal feelings toward the boy. But, Wattles, it doesn't affect the fact that Kemble disobeyed the regulations flagrantly. I was obliged to discipline him, and even so I let him off a good deal easier than I might have—possibly should have! The deuce of it is that, having learned this, I'm bound to feel rather a blighter for having punished him!"

"Well, sir, you didn't know," reminded Wattles.

"No, and now that I do know I'm afraid it can't alter things any. You understand that, Wattles?"

"Well, sir, asking your pardon," replied Wattles, "I'd like to say that, as I understand it, the law recognizes mitigating circumstances. I've been reading a bit of law, sir, this winter," he added apologetically.

"Granted, but the judge should also be unswayed by personal—er—feelings. The fact that Kemble disobeyed the rules out of—well, let us say loyalty to me, Wattles, ought not to affect my decision."

"Oh, absolutely not, sir!"

"Well, then, there we are." Mr. Connover smiled gently.

"Quite so, sir. When I suggested mitigating circumstances I had in mind the fact that Mr. Tom had the—the quarrel forced on him, Mr. Connover. He refused to engage with the other gentleman at that time and place, sir. It was not until the other young gentleman insisted and struck him, sir, that Mr. Tom—er—consented."

"Oh," said Mr. Connover, and then: "Oh, I see," he added thoughtfully. "Hm. Yes, there's that, isn't there?" And, after another pause: "Look here, Wattles, if I were you I'd keep on reading law," he said. "I honestly would!"

"Thank you, sir. I've been considering the study of it."

"Fine! Now suppose you go on with the case. Suppose you were in my place, Wattles, eh?"

"It's very kind of you, sir, to give—to receive my—"

"Not at all. What is your idea of the situation that exists at present? Frankly, after what you've told me I'd be mighty glad to reverse my decision if I could see an honest way to do it."

"Well, Mr. Connover, as I look at it, it's the other young gentleman who should bear the—the brunt of the punishment."

"Well, yes, it does look that way. In other words, I should have excused Kemble for the day and dropped Coles from the squad. I'm afraid I didn't give either of them a fair chance to explain what had occurred. Not, however, that Coles appeared anxious to do any explaining. Of course, if I did drop Coles now it would look a bit—well, odd. Belated justice, eh?"

"Yes, sir. And tomorrow being the last day of school, sir—"

"True." Mr. Connover's eyes twinkled, and he seemed to be enjoying himself hugely. "On the other hand, Wattles, there's no reason why I shouldn't, considering the mitigating circumstances, reduce the sentence inflicted on Kemble, which I now see was excessive, to—well, to forty-eight hours—or thereabouts. Does that sound correct?"

"Oh, absolutely, sir," replied Wattles gravely.

"Then," went on the coach, pursuing his thoughts, "with both Kemble and Coles in good standing on the team it only remains to determine which of the two in my humble opinion is likely to best fill the position of second baseman.

Wattles, you have cleared up a difficult position beautifully, and if we should be fortunate enough to win tomorrow you may take a large share of the credit to yourself. In fact, Wattles, to use an expression current about the campus, I've got to hand it to you!"

Mr. Connover arose and held out his hand. Wattles, seriously embarrassed, took it.

After supper the Triumvirate met as usual, and, as usual, Mr. Cooper joined the gathering before long. Clif arrived still depressed, although a hearty supper had somewhat leavened his woe. Before long he was taking a far less tragic view of his guilt, for Tom and Loring went to some pains to prove that, even if he had erred, he was not chargeable with the loss of the game.

"Suppose you'd caught the ball," said Loring. "That would have made only the second out, and one of those runs would have crossed in any case; probably both of them, for those guys reached the plate only about four yards apart. But even if your throw-in had nabbed the second, Wolcott would still have beaten us by one run."

"As far as that goes," declared Tom, "if the infield hadn't gone flooey those runners would never have been on bases! You should worry over dropping a fly after three infield errors had been chalked up!"

"Still, it was an awful thing to do," said Clif rather more cheerfully. "I—I don't know yet how it happened. I *caught* the ball all right, but, gee, somehow—"

"You were too anxious to make the throw," said Tom. "I've seen the same thing happen lots of times. Forget it, old son, and make up for it tomorrow."

"I will if I get the chance," sighed Clif, "but I guess Steve isn't likely to let me play tomorrow."

"Oh, I don't know. He needs hitters, Clif, and you're certainly hitting better than Al Greene."

"I didn't do much yesterday except for that one single."

"Say, how do you get that way?" demanded Tom. "My Sainted Aunt Jerusha, didn't that hit send in two runs? You're cuckoo!"

Wattles, who was already sorting out Loring's wardrobe for packing on the morrow, said no word when, later, Tom remarked dolefully: "Heck, I wish I were going to be in that rumpus tomorrow. I'll just bet I could knock the tar out of that Osterman guy! I'll bet I've got his number all right now!"

There was no study hour these evenings, and the conclave in Loring's room continued almost to bedtime, and as often as the talk wandered away from the final game with Wolcott just so often it switched back again before many minutes. That game was the principal subject of debate that evening all through the school, and even the enthralling occupation of packing up for departure Thursday morning was everywhere interrupted while the question of whether Steve would pitch Ogden or Frost or whether Cobham would be back of the plate was thrashed out.

While Wattles was massaging Loring that night the latter emerged from a period of silent abstraction to say: "Wattles, you said once you were pretty sure you had seen Mr. Cooper before. Remember?"

"Yes, sir."

"Well, did you ever happen to remember about it?"

"Yes, sir."

"You did! Well, why the dickens didn't you tell me?"

"Possibly the opportunity didn't occur, Mr. Loring."

"Opportunity my eye! You've had heaps of opportunities. I say, don't bear down so plaguy hard! Where was it you saw him, Wattles, and how'd you happen to remember?"

"It came to me one evening, sir, when I was cleaning some of your cravats. Mr. Cooper said he wasn't an American, if you'll remember, but an Englishman."

"Sure, I remember that, and how surprised I was."

"Yes, sir, so was I, for if I may say so the gentleman wouldn't strike one as a Britisher, doubtless owning to his having been away from England so much, sir. It was when he said that that I remembered the occasion of our former—that is to say, the occasion when I had seen him before."

"Really?" asked Loring interestedly. "Go on, Wattles. Shoot the works."

"I beg pardon, sir?" said Wattles startledly.

"Meaning tell the whole story," laughed Loring.

"Very good, sir, though there's not much to tell. I may not have mentioned it to you before, Mr. Loring, but the reason I came to this country was the War."

"The War! No, you never told me that, Wattles."

"Yes, sir. You see, they wouldn't have me on account of my eyes. Myopia they called it. I tried to get in twice, Mr. Loring, but I couldn't wangle it. I don't think folks were so unreasonable on this side, sir, but over there in England they made it frightfully uncomfortable for chaps like me. Slackers they called us, and worse than that, Mr. Loring. I couldn't stand it after a bit, and I came over here. But that's got nothing to do with what I started to tell you. After I'd been here about three years I happened down the avenue in New York, sir, and there was a gentleman, a British officer in uniform, making a speech from a platform. In Madison Square it was, I believe. Well, sir, I listened to him for quite a while. He spoke well. Told about what the Tommies and the others had to go through in the trenches, and put it fairly strong, sir. You understand, Mr. Loring, he was speaking for one of the Liberty Bond drives, as they called them. Well, sir, he put it over nicely, and there was a lot that heard him that dug right down on the spot. I remember there was a placard behind him that said 'Give Till It Hurts!' and he turned to it and said, 'That's the idea, men! Give till it hurts! Not you, mind! It's not you it will hurt! It's the enemy! Every dollar you loan to your Government hurts him! And you've got to go on hurting him until he can't stand it any longer! Give till it hurts!' Well, sir, maybe those weren't his exact words, but they're like what he said, and they hit hard, Mr. Loring. I'd bought two bonds, but I stepped up and I took another one, sir!"

"And that was Mr. Cooper!" exclaimed Loring.

"Yes, sir, that was him. A fine looking soldier he looked, too, Mr. Loring, and not till he'd finished his speech did I see that he had to use a crutch to walk back to the chair, sir."

"He'd been wounded, eh? Gee, that's interesting! And I'm sort of relieved, Wattles, because I rather gathered from the way you spoke that when you saw him before he wasn't—well, that there was something a bit off-color about him."

"Yes, Mr. Loring, I felt that way about it myself; rather as if the gentleman was connected with some unpleasant incident. Memory's a very odd thing, sir. You see, I didn't want to buy that bond; leastways, I did and I didn't, Mr. Loring, if you understand me. I thought I couldn't afford it, sir, but then, talking like he did, I couldn't help buying it. Maybe I had that in my mind, do you see? Not wanting to buy that bond and him just making me! Likely, Mr. Loring, that was where the unpleasantness—er—came into it!"

"Wattles," chuckled Loring, "you're a scream."

"Yes, sir," replied Wattles. "The other leg, please, sir."

CHAPTER XXII
THE FINAL GAME

GRADUATION DAY WAS ALL that it should have been as regarded weather. The morning was warm, but there was a fresh breeze from the southwest that stirred the maples along the village streets. Long before the exercises commenced the vicinity of the school was thick with cars, the Inn overflowed with visitors, and the little town had assumed the festal look that it wore once each year in June. The day belonged, of course, to the first class fellows, and they were much in evidence, some thirty-two in all, looking usually a bit self-conscious, sometimes rather self-important. The exercises were held out of doors on the lawn, the platform set against a background of trees, the settees ranged in semicircles before it. The scene was a fair one, colorful with the dresses of mothers and sisters and aunts dotting a lawn of emerald, with the bluest of blue skies above. One by one the graduates stepped to the platform and received their diplomas from Doctor Wyndham, shook the Doctor's hand and turned to face a salvo of cheers from their fellows. An orchestra, hidden by the branches, played softly. The Doctor made his address, and Mr. Clendennin, Head of the Junior School, spoke. Then came the announcement of the prize winners, and finally a prayer. Clif, who had volunteered as a "roustabout," hurried away to help a score or so of other boys prepare the assembly hall for the buffet luncheon to be served to the guests. There were long trestles to be set up, settees to be borne back from the lawn, a dozen other duties to be performed.

After luncheon the Doctor held a reception that lasted until half-past two, but Clif had nothing to do with that and set forth in search of Tom. The latter, though, was not to be found. Clif suspected that he had gone back to the Inn with Mr. Cooper after the exercises and had taken lunch there. He gave over the search at last and went up to his room and spent half an hour packing, he and Walter Treat getting horribly in each other's way during the operation. At two he made his way to the gymnasium, decorated with gay bunting and flowers for the school entertainment and dance to be held that evening, and found the elusive Tom in the locker room getting into baseball togs.

Clif stared a moment in surprise. Then he gave a shout of joy that brought inquiring looks from the few other early arrivals. "You're going to play!" he cried. "Say, that's great! How'd it happen? Gee—"

"Let go of me and shut up," said Tom, grinning. "Some one went and spilled an earful to Steve. I don't know who it was. I thought it might be Wink, but he swears it wasn't. Anyway, Steve said he'd been a bit too rough, and he guessed I'd been punished enough and told me to report for practice. He didn't say he was going to let me play, but Wink thinks he is. Tough on Wink, but he acted mighty decent about it. Says he's only getting what's coming to him. A pretty nice guy, that fellow, Clif."

Further remarks were prevented by the arrival of Hurry Leland. He had to shake hands with Tom earnestly, clap him on the back and punch him playfully in the ribs. "The million dollar infield again, Tom!" he chortled. "There's nothing to it, fellows! It's all Dark Blue!"

The rest of the team drifted in, heard the news and acclaimed it loudly. A quarter of an hour later they were out on the scrub diamond beginning an easy practice. Wolcott was already in evidence and the nearer stand had a brown tinge, although the game was not to start until three. After twenty minutes of work Coach Connover led the squad to a corner of the second team stand and talked to them a few minutes. Finally he read the batting-list: Tyson, 3B; Raiford, R.F.; Leland, S.S.; Bingham, C.F.; Talbott, L.F.; Kemble, 2B; Van Dyke, 1B; Cobham, C; Ogden, P.

"Let's play this game steady, fellows," ended the coach. "Make everything sure. Squeeze the ball every time you get it. If you do that, and hit the way you can hit when you make up your minds to, you'll get the game, the series and the championship. No cheers, fellows. Let's go."

Wolcott retired from the first team diamond, and Wyndham took possession for five minutes amidst the wild applause of the crowded stand. In practice the "million dollar infield" showed wonderful form, and more than once Captain Leland, Tyson, Van Dyke or Tom pulled stunts that brought approval from the spectators. There was plenty of speed and vim today. Finally a short man in the traditional blue serge of his profession waved his mask and addressed the stands.

"La—dies 'n gen'mun! Batteries for the game! For Wolcott, Osterman 'n Bailey! For Wyndham, Ogden 'n Cobham! Play ball!"

It was the Wolcott captain and center fielder who started the scoring, in the first half of the second, with a clean hit past Hurry. He was advanced on a sacrifice, pitcher to first baseman, took third on a sacrifice fly to left field and scored on a hit over second. Wyndham tied the game up in the same inning, however. Clif, first of the Dark Blue to face Osterman in that frame, hit to third baseman who fumbled badly. With three balls and one strike on Tom, Clif got the signal and set out for second. Tom swung, but missed, and Bailey, the Brown's catcher, pegged to the base. Clif slid under the ball safely. Tom struck out on the next delivery.

Talbott, following Tom at bat, reached first on an error, this time by second baseman, and on the throw to first Clif scuttled to third. The Wolcott infield appeared pretty well demoralized then. Talbott made an easy pilfer of second, the catcher making a short throw in hopes that Clif would try to score. But there was only one away and Clif hugged the bag. Van Dyke, after getting in the hole, began lifting fouls, and when he had sent right fielder twice across the line after them he managed to put the next fly fair. Clif brought in the tying run while the ball was being relayed to the plate. Cobham ended the inning with a strike-out.

In the next inning Ogden passed the third Wolcott batsman, but with two down he wasn't risking much. The subsequent man flied out to Tom. Wyndham proved that she had lost her awe of Osterman by getting two hits in her half. Pat Tyson made the first, after Jeff Ogden had fanned, and stole second on the next pitch. Raiford flied to short center and made the second out. Captain Leland advanced Tyson to third and went to first on a hit through the box. Clif, however, had no luck this time, and his easy grounder to Osterman was fielded for the third out.

Clif got his first chance in the field when Wolcott's shortstop selected Ogden's first offering in the fourth and crashed it well toward the running track. Clif had determined to follow Mr. Connover's instructions and "squeeze them" today, and when this ball landed in his hands he did his best to push it out of shape before he returned it to the infield. The previous batter had hit to first baseman for an easy out, and now, with two away, the next man secured Wolcott's third bingle by poling a fast one into left field. When, however, he tried to go down to second Cobham's perfect throw caught him standing up.

Talbott got his first hit in the last of the fourth, a Texas Leaguer back of shortstop, but he, too, was caught stealing. Tom hit a long fly to right for the second out, and Van Dyke fouled to first baseman. The game was going fast and honors were so far about even. Each team had scored once and each had three hits to its credit. Only in the matter of errors did Wyndham have the better of the argument, for the Dark Blue still had a clean slate while Wolcott had two miscues scored against her. There were thrills in every inning, and excitement was more intense than at either of the previous contests. Loring, seated today in the stand between Mr. Cooper and Wattles, had a simply frightful time with his scoring. Scoring calls for a steady hand and a cool head, and today Loring possessed neither!

But three men faced Ogden in the fifth, and but three faced Osterman. Each pitcher accumulated a strike-out, Jeff his first one of the game. In the sixth Wolcott started with the head of her list at bat. Ogden fanned him, however. The Wolcott left fielder smashed one at Tom and Tom tried hard to get it. He failed to reach it, though, by somewhat less than a foot and the ball traveled out to Raiford for a hit. Tom pulled down an easy fly and Talbott got under another.

Raiford swung hard at Osterman's first delivery but missed it. Osterman coaxed him with two wide ones and then sent one about waist-high, and Raiford shortened his grip and laid down a pretty bunt that placed him on first by the skin of his teeth. Hurry sacrificed with a slow one to shortstop. As Raiford had started for second with a big lead he was safe before second baseman was in position to take a toss and the ball went to first for the out. Clif found his batting eye and smashed out a pretty liner to left field for two bases, scoring Raiford. On Tom's out, second to first, Clif went to third and tallied when Talbott got his first hit which bounced off second baseman's shins. Talbott himself was thrown out when he tried to steal.

Wyndham celebrated those two runs with some of the loudest, most riotous shouting ever heard on the field. With a two-run lead it seemed that the game was as good as won! And Wolcott offered nothing in her half of the seventh to throw doubt on the assumption. The "million dollar infield" disposed expeditiously of the first two batsmen and Raiford of the third. Wyndham arose for the lucky seventh, cheered, stretched and remained standing while Van Dyke went out; first baseman to pitcher, Cobham lost his race to the bag by inches against shortstop's peg and Ogden lifted a fly to center fielder. Wyndham sat down again only mildly disappointed. Two runs was two runs!

Wolcott threw a scare into the Dark Blue's camp in the first half of the eighth when, with one down, Osterman seemingly decided to do his bit toward winning the game. The Wolcott pitcher had been at bat twice before, and had been thrown out at first each time. Now, however, he let Ogden get himself in the hole and then straightened out the fifth delivery for a two-bagger into right field. Had Osterman been satisfied with two bases the final score might have been different, but he rashly tried to stretch what was a generous two base hit into a skimpy three with the result that Raiford's throw to Hurry Leland and Hurry's fast peg to Tyson landed the ball at third while the Wolcott pitcher was still a yard from his goal. Wyndham breathed deeply with relief and yelled uproariously. The third man was an easy out, Hurry to Van Dyke.

Wyndham again failed to hit in her portion of the inning, Tyson, Raiford and Leland falling victims to the infield. Then Wolcott went to bat in what was presumably to be the final inning, Wyndham took the field confidently and cheerfully and the less enthusiastic fans prepared to depart.

CHAPTER XXIII
BASES FULL!

"FIRST MAN!" SHOUTED HURRY.

"First man!" echoed Van. "Let's get him, gang!"

"No one reaches first!" proclaimed Pat Tyson. "Go after him, Jeff!"

So Jeff nodded, wound up and pitched, and the Wolcott left fielder met the ball with his bat and sent it right back over Jeff's head and the trouble began. A reddish-haired lad named Quinn, who officiated at third base for the visitors, conferred with the Wolcott coach and advanced to the plate. He was evidently determined to make a sacrifice bunt and so Cobham signaled for low ones. With a strike and a ball scored, Quinn lifted one behind Van Dyke and just inside the foul line. Before the excitement was over there was a runner on second and a runner on first and no one was out!

Mr. Connover signaled along the bench and Erlingby and Frost pulled on their gloves and, followed by Gus Risley, retired behind the stand. The next man hit the ball across the diamond to Hurry, who, finding it too late for a play at second, sped the sphere to Van Dyke for the first out. A third hit followed, though, and the runners from third and second scored the tying runs!

Ogden threw out the next batsman at first, passed the subsequent one and then, while Wolcott still cheered and shouted and waved, made the third man raise an easy fly to Hurry Leland, bringing to an end a painful session!

Wyndham came in and went into conference about the coach. The score was 3 to 3. One run would settle the matter here and now, but whether that one run could be produced, and how, was a subject for thought. Clif was first up, and, after listening intently to words of wisdom from Coach Connover, faced an extremely composed looking Osterman. Steve had told Clif to wait for a pass and this he proceeded to do. But Osterman wasn't issuing passes yet, and after two strikes had been called against him and only two balls had been wasted by the pitcher Clif knew it was up to him to watch his step. The next delivery might have been intended for a drop, but it held pretty level and Clif got it fairly. The ball shot across the diamond a few feet to the left of the middle bag, and Clif was safe on first.

Tom Kemble, due for a sacrifice, had been told to hit it out, and he proceeded to do so. He let Osterman put the first delivery over for a strike and the second for a ball. Then he selected the next and whanged it down the third base line. There was a good deal of luck in that hit, but it served its purpose, which was to put Clif on second and Tom on first. In fact, Clif might have gone to third on it, and was well on his way when the coacher turned him back.

Talbott tried hard to get his second hit of the day then, but, although he fouled the ball all over the place, escaping being caught out by so many miracles, his final effort was a bounder to third baseman, and his heroic race to the bag failed of success. Van Dyke, who followed, was wildly implored to hit a home-run—although a single would have answered quite as well—and seemed willing to oblige. But Osterman for once failed to find the plate. Perhaps it was time he let down a bit, for he had pitched fine ball for eight innings. Two balls, a strike and two more balls, pitched while the Wyndham stand yelled and jeered in the universal manner of baseball crowds, sent Van to first and the bases were full!

Bases full and only one away! A hit would win the game and the championship! Coach Connover nodded to Sim Jackson and the umpire announced the substitution impressively. Sim looked decidedly nervous as he swung his bat and awaited the first offering, but determination shone through the nervousness, and after Osterman had twice missed the plate he took courage. Osterman worked a pretty drop over for a strike and duplicated the proceeding a moment later. Evidently the booing and shouting from the Wyndham stand were no more than music to his ears! Then Sim hit. The ball rose in a weak infield fly that dropped fairly into the third baseman's glove, while all three runners hurried back to their bases. Sim went back to the bench looking very woebegone. Two away now!

"Risley batting for Ogden!" shouted the umpire.

Gus could hit, and the Wyndham supporters took hope once more. But Gus could not, it appeared, hit today. Osterman fooled him badly on an out-curve, offered him a palpable ball that Gus almost went after in his anxiety and then scored again with a drop. As Gus recovered his balance after whirling around on one foot, Captain Leland, coaching at third, stooped and patted both palms against the sod. Clif took a deep breath, edged another foot from the bag, another—

Osterman was smiling a bit disdainfully as he took a short wind-up for the fourth delivery, but the smile faded abruptly. Along the path from third base a blue-stockinged form was speeding as though shot from a cannon. Cries of shrill warning sounded above the unceasing noise from the stands. Osterman stepped forward and shot the ball toward the plate, every ounce of strength behind it. Bedlam broke loose as runner and ball raced for victory. Bailey dropped despairingly, but the ball hit the dust in front of the rubber, struck his mitt and caromed off it just as Clif hurtled to the plate in a "fallaway" slide, an eager foot reaching for its goal!

The umpire, a squat figure in a cloud of yellow dust, held his hands down just as Bailey found that he was sitting on the ball. Clif struggled to his feet to discover himself in a mob of maniacal youths seemingly bent on his destruction. But they only shoved and tugged and boosted at him until he was swaying dizzily, and certainly insecurely, above the rabble. There was a fearsome din and lots of dust, and his captors, red-faced youths with wide-open mouths, seemed content to just mill around in the center of that increasing mob. But Clif was not the only one who was viewing the scene from above, for there was Captain Leland and Van Dyke and Tom, and every moment some other hero was lifted in air. Clif tried to wriggle loose, but his bearers only held him the tighter. Cheering began. Clif relaxed and grinned. It came to him that all this was eminently proper after all. They had won a mighty victory.

Tom had received a letter from his guardian that forenoon, but as it had reached him almost simultaneously with his restoration to the baseball squad he had not even opened it. Now, in Loring's room after supper, the talk finally veered from the afternoon's victory and Loring asked: "Your father isn't coming for you, is he, Clif?"

"No," was the answer. "He's in Chicago and doesn't get back until tomorrow evening. He's sending the car by a man from the garage. I'm going to drive it back, though!"

"Trust you!" said Tom. "What time do we start along, Loring?"

"Father said they'd get up here by eleven. That's about as early as they can make it. We'll stop for lunch somewhere, I suppose."

"Sure I won't be in the way?"

"Of course you won't. The car seats seven, and Wattles will sit in front. There'll be just the four of us behind. How about your trunk? Want Wattles to look after that in the morning? We're sending our stuff by express."

"Suits me. It's mighty nice of you to take me along, and the best of it is that I'll be ahead the price of the railway fare, and when you don't get much coin, anyway—" Tom stopped abruptly and slapped his pockets. "Heck, I almost forgot the old coot's letter! Came this morning and I stuffed it away— Here it is. Mind if I see how much he's made the check for?"

"Go ahead," said Loring. "Hope he's been generous."

"If he has," murmured Tom, "it's the first time—" He relapsed into silence, a slip of buff paper dangling from one hand and the accompanying letter in the other. Loring and Clif resumed conversation quietly. Suddenly there was an exclamation of dismay from Tom. "Well, what do you know?" he gasped. "The blamed old fish says I can't come back!"

"Come back?" echoed Clif. "Do you mean *here*?"

Tom crumpled the letter savagely. "Yes! He's had my report, and he says— Oh, what's it matter what he says? The main thing is I'm through!"

"But—but that's crazy!" Loring protested. "You passed! He's just trying to throw a scare into you, I guess. He's bound to come around before fall, Tom."

"Is he?" growled Tom. "You don't know him! It's the money he's thinking of, the—the blamed old miser! Says it would be wasting money for me to return, that I'm getting no results for what it's costing. And it's my money, too! All right, all *right*! But he needn't think I'm going to clerk in a store, or something like that, by heck! I'm—I'll run away first! I don't care what—"

Tom's angry voice was stilled by a gentle tap on the door. The breeze had died away and the door had been left well ajar for the admittance of any stray breath of air stirring in the corridor. Before Loring could answer, the tip of a cane came into view, the door opened wider and Mr. Cooper entered. He was in dress clothes, and Clif's first thought was one of envy. Clif had viewed his own evening regalia in the mirror half an hour since and had been rather well pleased with what he had seen, but now he realized that dress clothes alone were not enough; it was the manner of wearing them that counted most! Even Tom forgot his wrath for a moment in approving appraisal of the newcomer, and Loring spoke his mind frankly.

"Gee, Mr. Cooper, you're some sheik!" he exclaimed.

Mr. Cooper smiled as he laid hat and stick on the foot of Loring's bed. "Thanks," he answered. "Fact is, fellows, I haven't had these togs on for so long that they feel deuced strange. You chaps look rather sheikish yourselves, it seems to me!" He took his accustomed chair and viewed Tom's lowering countenance inquiringly. "What's this about running away, old chap?" he asked.

"I forgot the door was open," muttered Tom. "It's Mr. Winslow, sir. He doesn't like the marks I got and says I can't come back in the fall."

Mr. Cooper's brows raised. "Really! Why, that *is* bad news, isn't it?"

"Rotten!" declared Clif. "We had it all fixed to room together, sir."

"Tom says it's the expense that's worrying the guardian," said Loring. "And it's Tom's money, too."

"And so you're going to run away," mused Mr. Cooper.

"I'm going in the Navy," declared Tom defiantly.

"Well, now look here, Tom. Just put the matter out of your mind. Perhaps I don't rate very high with you chaps as a prophet, but I'm really quite a remarkable one, and I prophesy, Tom, that you'll be back here in September. And the September after that again."

Tom stared doubtfully. Then he grinned. "I'd like to know where you get your dope," he muttered.

Mr. Cooper waved a thin brown hand. "We prophets don't give ourselves away, old chap. But—" and he spoke so gravely that even Tom was impressed—"I give you my word that I know what I'm talking about and that it'll be just as I say. How about it?"

Tom laughed doubtfully. "I don't see how— But, heck, sir, you make it sound real!"

"It is real. You've got nothing to worry about. Mr. Winslow is—er—Mr. Winslow is mistaken."

"I hope he finds it out!" said Tom.

"I'm quite certain he will. You may count on—"

"I beg pardon!" The interruption came from the doorway where a tall, heavily-built gentleman stood half revealed. "I see that I'm wrong. But you will kindly tell me where I can find Mr. Clendennin? I was directed, I thought, to this room, but—" The intruder's gaze traveled from one to the other of the four occupants and came to rest on Mr. Cooper. It was then that his apologetic explanation ceased abruptly and a look of great surprise came into his face. He pushed the door wider and took a step into the room. "By the Great Horn Spoon!" he shouted. "Jack Kemble!"

Mr. Cooper arose and stepped forward with outstretched hand. "Hello, Dick," he replied quietly but with evident pleasure. "No idea you were about." Very gently he urged the other back to the threshold.

"But what the dickens," went on the visitor, still pumping the hand he held, "are you doing here? I say, Ellen, you've heard me speak of Captain Kemble a hundred times. Jack, shake hands with my wife." To the bewildered trio in the room a momentary vision of a blue-gowned figure showed behind the men. "The last I heard of you—"

The door swung slowly shut and only a murmur of voices came from the corridor. The three boys stared at each other in puzzlement. Then Clif sank back into his chair, and Tom followed suit more slowly. The silence lasted a full minute. Then Loring said: "What did he call him, Clif? I thought he said—"

"He did!" burst out Tom. "'Jack Kemble'! What's it mean? Did he get our names mixed, do you suppose? But I never saw him before!"

"I have," said Clif. "I saw him this morning. His name's Murdock. He's got a boy in the Junior School, a sort of fat kid—"

"But he called Mr. Cooper 'Jack Kemble'!" persisted Tom. "I—I don't like it! It's spooky! That was my—my—"

The door opened again and Mr. Cooper reëntered. He was smiling faintly, but the smile was different, and he avoided Tom's troubled eyes as he went back to his chair. "Dick Murdock," he explained apologetically. "We were together for a time during the War. I hadn't seen him for a number of years. Hope we didn't—er—startle you."

"No, sir, not a bit," murmured Loring.

"What did he call you?" demanded Tom a trifle shrilly.

"Oh, that!" Mr. Cooper laughed lightly. "That *was* startling, wasn't it? Murdock was always a perfect ass when it came to remembering names. By the way, just what did he call me?"

"Kemble, sir," answered Clif.

"I thought it sounded like that, too. Odd, eh? I mean, a bit of a coincidence, wasn't it?"

Tom was leaning forward in his chair, staring frowningly. "I don't believe that!" he broke forth harshly. "What *is* your name? You've got to tell us!"

The half smile left the man's face. For a long moment he stared at the floor. Then he lifted his gaze to Tom's, met it squarely and answered.

"John Middenwill Cooper-Kemble," he said.

There was another moment of silence in the room, broken at last by Tom's voice, low and trembling.

"What—what are you to—me?" he faltered.

The half smile returned to the man's face, but it held no suggestion of amusement. It seemed, rather, the smile of one ruefully contemplating his own perplexities. But his eyes never left Tom's as he replied.

"I regret that this has had to happen just now," he said quietly. "I hadn't meant it to. But you've a right to know." His voice fell to a gentler tone and he added deprecatingly, "I am your father."

———— ·◇· ————

"Of course," said Loring a few minutes later, when he and Clif were alone, "we ought to have guessed it long ago. After all, they're ridiculously alike, Clif."

"Alike? Gosh, I can't see that! And I don't see how anyone could have guessed—"

"I don't mean in looks, but in—in ways. Think, Clif. Forget their looks. Shucks, put another twenty years on Tom, and give him four of them in the

War, and he'd be Mr. Cooper—I mean Mr. Kemble—Mr. Cooper-Kemble—all over again."

"Do you think so?" asked Clif thoughtfully. "Yes, they are alike some ways. But I'd never have guessed they were father and son. And Tom told me about his dad, too, months ago. Gosh, I wonder—" Clif looked slightly alarmed.

"What?"

"He said he was going to tell his father what he thought about him if he ever found him, Loring! Do you suppose he will?"

Loring laughed. "I don't think you need worry about that. Tom's crazy about him, Clif. Has been for a month!"

Wattles entered, bearing a huge kit-bag from the storeroom.

"Look here," announced Loring, fearsomely, "you're not going to do any more packing tonight, Wattles. You're going over to the gym and see the show and have a good time. By the way, what time is it? We've got to be— Oh, I say, Wattles, here's a stunner! Who do you suppose Mr. Cooper is?"

"Mr. Cooper, sir?" Wattles set the bag down, dusted his hands carefully and allowed himself something that was almost a smile. "Mr. Cooper is Mr. Tom's father, Mr. Loring."

"*Wha-at!* How the dickens did *you* ever hear it?"

"I didn't exactly hear it, sir. I—er—I came to the conclusion by observation. Perhaps, sir, you'll recall Mr. Cooper leaving a leather cigar case behind him one afternoon."

"No, I don't, but what about it?"

"I took the liberty, sir, of examining it. Not from any desire to—er—pry into the gentleman's affairs, sir, but merely because I have a—a weakness, as you might say, for leather articles—"

"That's all right! Get on, Wattles, for Pete's sake!"

"Yes, sir. Well, Mr. Loring, there was a name printed under the flap; in gold letters, sir: 'J. M. Cooper-Kemble' it was."

"For the love of lemons!" sighed Loring. "How long ago was this, Wattles?"

"Perhaps a fortnight, sir."

"And you never said a word!"

Wattles drew himself up slightly. "I am not the sort, Mr. Loring, to violate a gentleman's confidence," he replied with dignity.

Loring threw up his hands. "You'll do, Wattles! Here, get me over to the gym. It's eight o'clock already!"

It was nearly three hours later when Clif found Tom again. He might not have found him then if he had not withdrawn from the gymnasium for a breath of air. Tom was sitting alone on a step at the bottom of the flight. Clif called to him and he turned and answered dreamily: "Oh, that you, Clif? Great night, isn't it?"

"Yes." Clif went down and seated himself at Tom's side. After a moment, during which Tom seemed to have forgotten his chum's presence in silent contemplation of a shining half moon Clif asked diffidently: "Is everything all right, Tom?"

"Eh? What did you— Oh, you bet! Listen, I'm to come back next fall, Clif, and right along until I'm finished, no matter if it takes ten years! He said so. And I'm to go to college, too! And next summer— Say, it wasn't bunk at all, about us getting together in Switzerland! It's real! We're going to do it, Clif! I'm going abroad with him; for all summer; France, Germany, Switzerland—hundreds of places! Gosh, isn't that wonderful? Why, this morning I never expected to see anything all my life but just New Jersey!"

"Gee, that's simply corking!" cried Clif, thrilled. "And, I say, Tom, you didn't—didn't talk to him like you said you were going to, did you?"

Tom shook his head. "I couldn't do it. I don't know just how it was when I was a kid and he went away, but he told me a little. You see, his father died—I forgot to tell you we're pretty well off, he and I, Clif!—and he had to go across; back to England; and mother—well, she didn't want to go; anyway, she wouldn't. And father sent for her and—and she still wouldn't go to him—I suppose folks don't all get along very well together, even if they are married, Clif. Anyway, father didn't see her again. He meant to. He meant to come back, but he went to Africa, and then the War broke out. Oh, I guess he was to blame, all right, but—well, a fellow doesn't want to say anything against his mother, especially when she's dead, Clif. And she was a mighty fine mother to me; and he says she was fine, too. Only—well, they didn't seem to get along. He didn't know she had died until a whole year after. And when he tried to find me he couldn't for a long time. He wasn't going to tell me about being my father yet, he says. He wanted to—to make sure that—that I wanted him, you see. He said tonight that it needn't make any difference. That if I wasn't ready to have him for a father he'd leave me alone until I was."

Tom paused and the music from the dance floor came out in a sudden flood of melody. The white moon, momentarily hidden by a fleecy purple cloud, sailed forth again.

"What did you tell him, Tom?" asked Clif anxiously.

Tom, staring up at the moon, grinned almost embarrassedly.

"I told him," he answered, "that he'd better stick around!"